The Cursed Heir

The Frost Series

Book 1

Adam Schrag

For my grandpa, the original storyteller

Chapter One

Everyone claims they didn't start the chain of events that leads to them discovering they're not from Earth, but I need to stress this to you anyway: *They* found *me*. I didn't know the place I came from existed, and I wanted nothing to do with it, either, but family has a way of changing things. At least it came with a cool nickname.

My name is Jaden. That's all you need to know for now, because, well, if you happen to be a part of this, too, you have to pick who you're fighting for. If I told you more, it could put us both in danger. That's why I'm serious when I say this: I'm trusting you with this.

I need to start at the beginning, otherwise none of this will make sense. I'll start the morning of my freshman year. My life before that? You'll hear about it, eventually.

Here's where it all changed.

I was already awake when Rose, or "Mom," as she demanded

I call her, pounded on my bedroom door for the second time. I'd been awake the first time, too, not that it mattered.

"Jaden, get up! It's your first day, and your father and I are about to leave," she yelled through the door.

"Where to this time?" I mumbled, throwing my feet over the edge of the bed. Paris? No, that was May. California? June. Or was it July?

She threw the door open, barged into the room, and opened the curtains, allowing blinding light to flood the room. My eyes cried out in protest, and I quickly shielded them from the onslaught.

"Ellen will be here any second. She's taking Oliver, and your bus picks you up on the corner. Now, get a shirt on and go eat breakfast," she said as she left, heading toward Oliver's room, yelling something about how the adoption agency told her boys would be easier to take care of than girls.

I got dressed to go downstairs. The school I was being sent to had a uniform policy, but I refused to wear it a minute longer than I needed to. Instead, I threw on a hoodie despite it being a Monday in early August here in Washington, DC. I'd never been bothered by temperature. It's like my body forgets to react to it, and I push it aside the same way I did almost everything else in my life.

I headed down the hall to the bathroom, nearly running over Oliver as he left his room. He wasn't as ready for his first day of school, still wearing the gray tank top and boxers he had slept in.

His tired amber eyes lit up when he saw me, and the goofy smile I'd grown to love beamed across his face.

"Jaden, it's our first day of actual school!"

"Hey, Ollie." I ruffled his messy bed-headed mop of black hair. "You need to get changed before Rose comes back up here and makes you go in your pajamas."

Ollie laughed as he ran back into his room to get ready.

Ollie is my brother. At least that's what I call him, and nobody is going to change that. Technically, we aren't related. He's ten years old, five younger than me. We met in the fourth foster home I'd been placed in by the time I was thirteen. I, like him, never knew my real parents. According to my first foster parents, I was dropped off on the doorstep by a middle-aged woman. "His name is Jaden Frost," she said before handing me off and disappearing forever. I was only days old at the time. It was my first time moving to a different house, but it certainly wouldn't be my last.

I made it until I was nine before my first parents, the Days, couldn't handle me anymore. Maybe it was the attitude; maybe it was the fighting. I never went looking for a fight, but I always ended up in them. When you get placed in a house with four other boys, all of whom are looking to be the parents' favorite, it's bound to happen.

And I won those fights. All of them, at least when it wasn't four against one. I had a sixth sense when it came to fighting, even when I was little. Sure, I might've been up against a twelve-year-old who had no fighting experience, but they always ended with me on top. It's like I could predict his every move, dodging them and showering him with weak punches in return. But eventually, I did enough damage.

The other boys always sided against me. It would take all of them, but they would wrestle me to the ground, hammering my face with punches until I cried and my nose bled all over my shirt. It only took a couple of these occurrences before the Days shipped me to the next house.

My time there was short-lived. Only a couple of weeks, in fact. After multiple fights, I was moved to the Alvarez's house.

Mr. and Mrs. Alvarez ran a large foster-care house, taking care of twelve of us. They never had any intention of adopting any of the children, instead looking for good parents for us to be placed with long-term. At times, it felt more like an orphanage than a home.

Despite that, Mr. Alvarez was the first adult to welcome me with open arms. He treated us all well, doing his best to be the father-figure we needed. He'd cook for us, drive us all to the local elementary school we went to, and help us with homework in the evenings. I did my best to stay out of fights, only getting into a few.

What I looked forward to most was Friday nights. The Alvarez house was surrounded by a massive backyard, with plenty of space for all the kids to run around. With twelve of them, nine of them boys, the Alvarez house was the place to be. The entire neighborhood would show up to the house for the weekend wiffle ball games, which we played well into the late hours.

I was never the best, but it's where I started to dream of one day making the high school baseball team. I imagined myself in the batter's box, the outfield, even pitching. I was the only left-handed player, so it was a good thing we didn't use gloves for our games. We already didn't have enough for everyone, but there were zero left-handed ones.

My wiffle ball career ended the day I was adopted. I was twelve, and they were the best parents I could've asked for. They were younger, sure, but they treated me like the son they'd always wanted. I did all I could to be the perfect kid. And I thought I was pretty good at it.

Do you ever get the feeling that things are going too well and something horrific is bound to happen? Well, I hadn't developed that awareness yet, but when I stood all alone on the front doorstep of the Alvarez's house as they drove away, I developed it fast. I shut everyone out of my life after that.

I spent a couple of days with Mr. and Mrs. Alvarez before, once again, I was sent to a different house. I had begged them not to make me go, but it was useless.

"I'm truly sorry, Jaden, but it's for the best," Mr. Alvarez said once the car to take me away arrived. He made me promise him I would stay out of fights, and I did, though I doubted I'd be able to keep it. Tears had rolled down my face as I got into the backseat. I think I even saw a tear on his cheek as we pulled away.

I was the second youngest kid at my fourth foster home, the Bishops, but I had by far the worst attitude. No matter how hard the parents or other kids tried to get close to me, I pushed them all away.

Almost. Ollie is the only one who managed to wiggle his way under the walls I had put up. He's always been an optimistic and cheerful person, which was heavily frowned on by the other kids. Especially by this tall, curly-haired kid named Barrett. He was my age, but that didn't stop him from picking on Ollie every chance he got. To make matters worse, he had his gang of equally ruthless older kids who de facto ran the place. Barrett gave me a hard time, too, of course.

He did his best to get under my skin. Even resorted to

shoving and punching me when I wouldn't respond to him. But I kept my promise to Mr. Alvarez, avoiding all fights. Maybe it was the promise; maybe I knew fighting would get me sent away, again, and I was tired of moving to different homes.

One day in particular, Barrett had his sights on me. He let me have it all morning, attacking a variety of aspects of my life, from my average height to the fact I didn't know who my parents were. He didn't know who his were, either, so I thought it was weird. It was around noon and Barrett had yet to get a response out of me, so with a huff, he moved on. Ollie had watched the entire exchange and made his way to the couch, sitting next to me.

"How did you do that?" he asked as he sat down. I didn't reply; instead, I just stared at him. He stared back at me, squinting his eyes mockingly, curling up his upper lip to seal it.

"This is what you did?" When I didn't respond again, he sighed. "Tough crowd."

I couldn't help it. I gave him a small smile and told him that if he really wanted to annoy Barrett, he should just stare at him that way.

Ollie attached himself to my hip after that. It was annoying at first, but he weaseled his way past the walls and the guardrails I'd developed. When we found out a year later that we would both be adopted to the same home, I felt like I was responsible for him.

I made my way downstairs for breakfast just as the doorbell rang. My adoptive dad, Dane, passed me as I reached the bottom of the stairs.

"Jaden, could you get that? It should be Ellen."

Ellen stood there when I opened the door. She is this older

woman Rose and Dane hired to make sure Ollie and I didn't wreck the house while they went on vacation. She looked like your stereotypical librarian: graying hair, pointy nose, always wore a pantsuit, and completed the look with those glasses that were held on her face by a chain. She was nice enough, so we didn't mind.

Today, however, she had someone else with her, a younger man, probably in his mid-twenties.

"Good morning, Jaden," Ellen said. "Are you ready for your first day at an actual high school?"

"Sure," I answered, stepping aside to let them in.

"Jaden, this is my son, Noah."

I nodded hello to him and turned to head to the kitchen.

"Doesn't he have just the most vibrant blue eyes? I wasn't lying to you," Ellen said, presumably to Noah.

"Yes, he does, and we couldn't be more proud of our son," Dane said as he appeared from around the kitchen corner.

Dane Edwards was the complete opposite of his wife, Rose. How they ended up together, I'll never know. His love for Ollie and me felt genuine enough, so although I didn't reciprocate it, I tried to act decent around him.

Still, I hate it when the conversation is about me, because generally, it only happened when I was in trouble. Yes, I have blue eyes. Like, very blue. My blond hair does nothing but provide even more contrast for them. Dane once described them as "the color of fresh ice in a blue ocean." Rose didn't talk to me for a whole day after that.

"I didn't know you had a son," Dane said now to Ellen.

"Oh yes, I must not have mentioned him before. He travels a lot, but he's finally in town."

"Well, it is nice to meet you, Noah, I believe it was? You're welcome to stay here with Ellen if you'd like."

They kept talking, but I decided I wasn't hungry anymore and climbed back upstairs to pack my bag for school. Something didn't feel right about Noah. I thought he was too young to be Ellen's son, but I pushed the thought aside.

Not long after, I was last off the bus at Pioneer Memorial High School, wearing the school uniform's khaki pants with a white button-up shirt and black tie, covered by a forest green sweater vest. Pioneer Memorial was a modern-looking two-story building about two miles from the Capitol building, right in downtown DC. Glass panels made up the front of the school, with banners exclaiming Welcome Back Students! strung high above the entrance. I could only imagine how much it cost the Edwards to send me here, which really made me mad, and I didn't know why. I hoped I could make it four years here, because, if nothing else, at least they had a baseball team.

Regardless, I was the new kid and could feel the eyes on me as I walked into the building. Giant stone sculptures of supposedly famous pioneers welcomed all who entered, but even they seemed to eye me differently.

I made my way past the figures and weaved through a massive foyer full of other students hanging out before the first day of classes. They all wore the same uniform, but in replacement of pants, the girls wore a khaki skirt. They sat in bunches, many around tables, and some even on the tables.

I'd memorized my schedule a week before. It was bad enough that I would be the new kid, I didn't need to get lost, too. First up was algebra with Mrs. Zimmer. I worked up the courage to ask one of the teachers who lined the halls looking for troublemakers, and after explaining to him I was new, he pointed me in the classroom's direction.

I'd almost made it when a voice erupted from behind me.

"Frosty!"

I stopped cold. I was thinking about how I'd never see him again when I was wrapped in a bear hug and lifted off the ground. Eventually, I was released, and I turned to face Barrett.

"Hey, buddy! It's been a while," he said.

I stared in bewilderment, not sure if he was real or some figment of my anxious imagination. "Y-yeah, sure has been."

"What class you got first? I've got math with some Zimmer lady."

Unbelievable.

"I have that, too," I whispered.

"No way! Let's go, then!"

Barrett led the way; I hung my head and followed.

I swear Barrett had every other class with me. Even if I could lose him between classes, he'd show up at the next one. In biology, which was the fourth and final class before lunch, he sat right next to me. The teacher, Mr. Irving, handed each of us a plant that had been grown in a milk carton. Apparently, we were supposed to be able to tell how photosynthesis worked from this, but focusing was difficult when Barrett kept commenting on how much shorter my plant was than his.

After the fourth comment, I touched my stupid plant, willing it to grow. To my horror and partial astonishment, it did. A new leaf formed where I touched it, the stalk of which grew slowly, but steadily. It wasn't much, but it was now just as tall, if not taller, than Barrett's. Barrett announced to the class that I'd stolen his plant, so Mr. Irving made me switch with him. I didn't dare try to make this one grow as well.

The only break I got was at lunch, which I ate by myself. Nobody wanted to share a table with the quiet and weird new kid who stole plants, and I didn't blame them one bit. When the last bell rang, I shot out of the school and hopped on my bus, ducking down into one of the back seats, terrified Barrett was going to be on it.

Barrett never got on, and soon the bus was stuck in downtown DC traffic. Despite the noise coming from the other kids, I could relax for the first time all day. I thought back to science and the plant, wondering if I'd made it grow, and how that was possible. I made zero progress by the time the bus arrived at my stop. After a short walk, I entered the house where Ellen, Noah, and Ollie watched a show on Nickelodeon.

"How was your first day?" Ellen asked.

"Interesting."

"Come watch with us, Jaden!" Ollie said, just his eyes peeking over the back of the couch.

"Yes, please do," Noah said now, turning around to face me. His look was intense, as if he was staring through me. It was unnerving, but I wanted to join them, so I made my way to the couch, taking a seat next to Ollie.

We sat watching cartoons for about fifteen minutes. I took a few handfuls of popcorn from a bowl Ollie held, and soon it neared empty. Before it could get there, Ellen hopped up, imploring Ollie to follow her to the kitchen to get more.

"But I'm not even done," Ollie protested, but Ellen dragged him off the couch by the arm.

Soon after they disappeared, Noah inched closer to me. I watched him, but I turned and faced him when he got within a foot.

"So, you're Ellen's son?" I asked, doing my best to act casual.

"Sure am. Have been all twenty-five years."

His stare was as intense as before. This time, however, it felt evil.

"Oh, nice."

This guy was beyond creepy, so I scooted away. I kept moving away from him, but I was soon up against the edge of the couch. He followed me.

"You know I'm only fifteen, right?" I asked jokingly, but he kept inching closer. When he was within a foot again, something in me snapped. "What are you doing?" I hoped Ellen would hear and come back.

"My job. Don't think we don't know who you are, Jaden Frost," he hissed.

For some reason, my brain didn't focus on him knowing my real last name.

"We?"

Before he could answer, the doorbell rang. Noah took his eyes off me for a second, but it was all I needed to launch myself past the side of the couch and take off for the door. He grabbed for my arm, but I pulled it away, leaving him with a fistful of air.

Chapter Two

Noah didn't chase me, which was a good thing. The front entrance to the Edwards' home is polished mahogany wood, and it's slick when wearing socks. After I missed the front door and ended up flat on my back attempting to stop, I scrambled to my feet and flung it open.

On the other side stood an older woman flanked by two teenagers. I checked back into the living room, but Noah was gone, so I turned to study the new arrivals.

On my far right was a dark-skinned guy slightly older than me. He was a couple inches taller and although I thought I was a pretty good fighter, this guy looked like he could've shredded me with his bare hands if he wanted to. His dark-green eyes matched the unzipped black and green jacket he wore, making him even more intimidating to look at. A silver chain with a small double-sided ax pendant hung around his neck.

The woman was in the middle. Of the three, she seemed the most out of place. She had on a simple, beige robe-like dress that went to the floor, but she was wrapped in a light blue cloak that was tied around her neck. She held onto a straight walking staff, though she didn't use it for balance. A shining blue orb rested on top of the staff. Clouds of white, that matched the color of her hair, floated in the orb. She looked at me with intense eyes, and I could tell she was the leader of the group.

There was a girl on the left. She had a curious look on her face, like she was expecting me to give her trouble. She rolled the sleeves up on her gray athletic jacket, revealing tanned skin that shimmered in the sunlight. Brown hair hung around her shoulders, matching her eyes. She wore a necklace, too, but hers was made of a thin, braided black rope and tucked down into her jacket, so I couldn't tell if she had a pendant on it. She frowned at me, but seemed to be the least likely to want to hurt me.

I stared at the trio in front of me. Nobody said anything for a moment.

"Jehovah's Witnesses?"

"Do we look like Jehovah's Witnesses to you, bro?" asked the taller guy on the right.

"I don't know, never seen one."

"It's him," the woman in the middle said.

I looked back at her. My face probably said a million things, but I'm not sure any of them gave any indication I knew what was going on.

The girl on the left squinted and tilted her head, studying my face.

"Are you sure? He had white hair and was taller in the phantom."

"That was just a guess. I would recognize those eyes. They're just like his father's."

Like my father's? Somehow, I got more confused. How did these people know my dad? Was he alive and out in the world? And why did I care? He abandoned me, not the other way around.

I was about to tell this old woman she had the wrong blue-eyed kid when a sound beside me stole my attention. Ellen appeared seemingly out of thin air, grabbed the collar of my school uniform, and threw me backward into the house with enough force that I would've thought it was the ripped teenager outside had I not seen her do it myself.

I ended up on my butt. Seriously, the socks gave me no traction. Ellen looked at me with a look that said, *You poor thing*, before calmly turning around, slamming the front door, and locking it. She straightened out her charcoal gray pantsuit before taking a deep breath and smiling at me. It was almost comforting. With a turn, she headed back to the kitchen. As she did so, she called out, "You two play nice!" before disappearing again.

You two play nice? Who was she… Noah. From my seated position, I looked around the living room, desperate to find him before I got blindsided. I spotted him at the base of the stairs, about fifty feet away, down the main hall. He had a wild look, but that was the least of my concerns—he held a long, silver dagger in his right hand. He walked toward me, slowly at first, but picking up speed with each step. I ripped the socks off my feet. As he approached, he flipped the dagger in his hand, catching it by the blade. The sixth sense that had helped me in every fight growing up kicked in, and I knew he was going to throw it. As he approached, he raised his arm above his head, just as I expected.

Thirty feet from me, Noah's hand started forward, the dagger ready to launch. As it did, my feet planted, and I dove backward, pushing off the ground with both my arms and legs to gain more distance. The dagger dug deep into the wood with a thunk right where I'd been a second ago. I landed on my back, again, but this time I used my momentum to roll up and over my shoulders, finishing the move by landing on one knee, ready to dive again if needed.

When did I learn to do that? I'm not one to brag, but it was pretty cool. In front of me, I could see the dagger, its tip buried deep in the floor. Rose was not gonna be thrilled when she saw the scratch that would leave. Noah was running now, and I knew he would beat me to the blade. I moved to put more distance, and the couch, between us. He arrived on the other side, the dagger back in his hand. I didn't figure he would throw it again; if he missed this time, I would beat him to it.

It wasn't your typical Mexican standoff. Noah scowled at me across the couch, but neither of us made a move. I'd never lost a fight before, but I was afraid that if I lost this one, it would be my last.

"You know, I'm starting to think you aren't Ellen's son," I said.

"What gave it away?"

"She's never tried to kill me."

"Pity. You're a little better when you're trying."

"Huh?"

His confidence scared me. All my other opponents had been as inexperienced as me, but this guy, whoever he was, knew what he was doing. I had just caught my breath when he leapt over the couch, clearing it easily. He swung the dagger as he landed, the tip snagging some of the fabric of my vest as I jumped out of the way. I ducked under another swing and went to leap back toward the front door. Noah recovered much faster than I anticipated, and a third swing nicked my calf as I jumped. The sharp pain threw off my trajectory, and I tumbled off the top of the couch and sprawled out on the floor.

I tried to scramble to my feet, but Noah tackled me before I could make it. A loud crash echoed through the house, but I was too focused on the blade swinging wildly around my head to pay it any attention. I would throw him off me to mild success, but every time he'd jump back on before I could move.

Each attempt took a little more out of me, and eventually one of his swipes caught me above the left temple. I felt warm blood trickle down my face. I tried to throw him off one last time, but he straddled me and didn't allow me to move. I knew I was in trouble.

Above me, Noah smiled. "Better, but not good enough."

"I don't think it was really fair that only you had the knife," I said.

He raised the dagger above his head, ready to stab down. I waited for whatever that sixth sense was to kick in again, but I think it was out of ideas, too.

The dagger started its downward arc when a blast of air sent him flying off me and both of us skidding across the floor. Noah got to his feet much faster than I could, but after a glance down the hall and a frustrated grunt, he bolted deeper down the hallway toward Rose and Dane's bedroom. The three people from the front door appeared next to me.

"Check on him. Vinny and I are going after the other one," the old woman said, the big dude, Vinny, right beside her. They rushed down the hall while the girl knelt over me.

"How bad are you hurt?"

Her big brown eyes bore into me. My calf didn't burn as much as my head, so I started with the obvious.

"His knife hit me here," I said, bringing my hand up to the cut. It hurt to touch, and my hand came away bloody. "My leg got cut, too, but it's not as bad."

She reached down and put her hand on my head. I winced in anticipation, but her hand was cool, and it helped with the pain.

"Do you want a scar or not?" she asked.

"Huh?"

"You're a boy, of course you want a scar."

She pressed down a little harder. A warm feeling flooded through my body, the sting from my calf disappearing. It traveled up, making its way to my head. The burning feeling from the cut relaxed, and what felt like a cool breeze replaced it.

Above me, the girl grimaced a little. "There, you're fine now," she stated matter-of-factly, pulling her hand away.

To my surprise, not a single drop of blood was on it. I touched where the cut had been with my clean hand, feeling only a small ridge. My hand returned with no blood on it as well. I touched the cut on my leg, but it was completely gone.

"How did you…? What? Where did it go?" I stammered.

"You can do it, too. You've got a lot to learn, Jaden."

So, I guess everyone knew my name.

She extended her hand and helped me to my feet. "I'm Maya Reed. The big guy is Vincent, as you may have heard. The woman is Lucinda."

As if summoned, Vincent and Lucinda returned from down the hall, Lucinda still holding her walking stick with the glowing sphere. Vincent now carried the double-sided ax he wore on his necklace, except it had grown to a full-size battle ax. A gray, metallic handle gave way to a rich, glimmering black blade that reflected the light no matter which way it turned. I could tell how sharp it was just from looking at it.

He must have seen me gawking, because he made a big show of brushing off the blade with his hand. "Like what you see?" he asked. "Her name is Windweaver, and she just saved your life."

As he said it, the weapon shrank in his hand until it was the size of the pendant. As he attached it back to his necklace, he said, "Bet you haven't seen that happen before."

I shook my head.

Vincent was about to say something else when his gaze moved to something behind me. "Hey, little man," he said.

I turned to see Ollie standing where the kitchen met the main hallway. He held a fresh bowl of popcorn, though he had stopped eating it while he stared at the odd scene in front of him.

"Hey, Ollie," I said. "Where's Ellen?"

He pointed back toward the kitchen but said nothing.

"Is she acting strange?"

He nodded. "She keeps making popcorn."

I walked into the kitchen, the three strangers and Ollie trailing behind. I was half-expecting Ellen to be waiting there to attack me, too, but the only thing I found was multiple bowls of popcorn, just as Ollie had said.

After a brief search, we found her asleep on the couch. I explained to the group how she had brought Noah with her today, claiming he was her son. I ended my explanation with the story of her surprising strength and weird actions.

"Noah broke a window and escaped before we could catch

him, but he had to have been a Desolate," Lucinda said, Vincent and Maya agreeing with her.

"A what?"

"A Desolate. It's one of the six powers you can get from Krera."

"Oh, that makes sense," I said, my voice dripping with sarcasm.

"You may be the Queen's son, but your mother would give me permission to smack you," Lucinda fired back.

"Lucinda, let me explain it to him," Maya said.

"Go for it, child."

Maya faced me. "Where do I begin?" She paused. "You're not a normal kid."

I think I would've started somewhere else. "What is that supposed to mean?" I asked, getting defensive.

"I mean you're not from this realm. You grew up here, but you weren't born here. You're from a place called Arrortha. It's a different realm from this one."

"And let me guess, you can only get there by portal?"

"How'd you know?"

"Okay. This has been fun. Haha, joke's on Jaden. Let's pretend he's from a different planet—"

"Realm," Maya interjected.

"Whatever. Did Barrett put you up to this?"

"Who? Look, Jaden, none of us—" She motioned to herself, Vincent, and Lucinda. "None of us are from this realm, either. Outside of Lucinda, none of us have been here before now. We were sent by your mother, I might add, to come find you and bring you back."

"My mother?"

"Yes. She sent you here to protect you."

"Protect me? From what?"

"Quite a lot, actually."

"None of this makes sense. How do you know who I am?" I asked.

"Because I'm the one who brought you to Earth when you were a baby," Lucinda said. "We've been looking for you for three months, ever since we learned you weren't at the home where I dropped you off. In fact, we tracked that Desolate until he led us right to you. It won't make sense for a while. We can explain more as we go, but right now it would be better if we weren't in the same place we were the last time they found you."

"Noah?"

"Look at you, you're already learning. Go pack what you might need for a couple of days. We've got some ground to cover to get back to the portal."

I tried to ask her a few more questions, but each time she interrupted me by declaring, "You need to go pack before I do it for you. And trust me, you won't like what I pack."

Frustrated, I grabbed my school bag on my way upstairs and emptied its contents onto my bed. Call it an educated guess, but I didn't think I'd be needing any of that stuff soon. I wouldn't leave the house without getting a few more answers out of somebody, but in case I went with them, I didn't think I would like whatever Lucinda threw in the bag.

After adding a few changes of clothes to the bag, I changed myself, putting on a plain white t-shirt and a pair of black jogger-style pants. I covered the t-shirt with a gray Adidas hoodie. Before heading back downstairs, I made a stop in Ollie's room and grabbed multiple changes of clothes for him. I didn't know if he was from this magical world as well, but no way would I leave him alone here with Ellen.

Back downstairs, the newcomers stood over the babysitter, who was still fast asleep on the couch.

"Is she all right?" I asked, joining them.

"She will be. That Desolate had control, but now that he's gone, she'll be fine after a while," Maya said.

This was going to be my best chance at getting some answers before we left, so I pressed.

"You mean he was controlling her?"

"Kind of. A Desolate's power makes someone see what they would usually try to ignore. Weaknesses, flaws, dark desires, stuff like that. They break you down over time, enough to where they can manipulate you into doing things. We don't know how long he had been working on Ellen, but she was very easily influenced, as you saw."

"Why did he do that to her? If he was after me, why didn't he just do it to me?"

Maya smiled at me. "Because you have the same power too, which makes you much more resistant to them."

"So I can do what Noah did?"

Her smile faded, her voice taking a more serious tone.

"Yes, but it comes at a cost. Most Desolates don't live with the other powers in Arrortha. All powers have a curse, and the more they use their powers against others, the stronger their powers grow against themselves. Most go insane by the time they grow old."

"They're cursed if they use their abilities?"

"All the six powers are, each in their own way."

"What power are you?" I asked her.

"Healing," she replied. "Or Medela. Whichever you prefer."

I looked at Vincent, and asked, "What about you?"

He puffed out his chest. "I'm all natural," he said.

"So, you don't have any powers?"

"I chose not to have any, and yes, there's a difference. Everything I do is done by me, not by gifted magic."

Lucinda stepped into the middle of the group. "You'll figure it out, but right now, we need to leave. We aren't the only ones looking for you."

"No. Why would I go with you? Because you claim my babysitter's psycho son had superpowers?" I asked. Nothing they were telling me sounded real, and my frustration was growing.

"I'm guessing he was trying to control you and take you back to Arrortha himself," Maya said.

"That's only slightly more comforting than what I thought was happening."

"When it was clear you were too strong for him to influence easily, he decided option two would be easier, so he tried to kill you. I understand how confusing this is," she added.

"Do you?"

"What do you have to lose?" Vincent challenged now. "This isn't your actual home; this isn't even your real family. Your real mother is alive and waiting for you. I know that alone interests you enough to think about going with us."

As much as I didn't want it to, it did.

Vincent said, "How about this? You go with us. If at any point you still feel like all of this is made up, you're welcome to leave and come back here. But trust me, once we start heading toward the portal, you won't want to."

When I still didn't respond, he kept going, but his voice softened.

"Look, I understand. You're confused and probably a little scared, too. It's all right. But I also know that you want more out of life than what you're getting. I know your type. You weren't born to waste away in a classroom learning about stuff you don't care about. Here's your chance, Jaden. A chance to get away from it and discover who you really are."

For the record, it was a good speech. For the record's record, I didn't buy it. But he was right. What did I have to lose? The only thing keeping me at the Edward's house was Ollie.

I asked, "Anytime I think it's all fake I can leave?"

"Anytime," Vincent said.

I pointed at Ollie now. "And he's going, too." It was a statement.

"Sure, little man can go if he wants."

I pulled Ollie aside and squatted down so I was eye level.

"What's happening, Jaden?" he asked me.

"I'm not totally sure. It sounds like I'm going on an adventure, but I don't want to go without you. Would you want to go with me?"

"What about Mom and Dad?"

"Rose and D— Mom and Dad are gone right now, so we have to be brave and go without them."

"Maybe they'll find us after!"

"Maybe they will, but right now, we'll have to protect each other. I know you can protect me. Do you think I can protect you?"

Ollie laughed, stood up tall, and said, "I can protect both of us."

I smiled at him and turned around to the others. "Anytime we want to, we can come back."

"Anytime," Vincent repeated.

* * *

Two minutes later we were ready to go. I asked Maya again if Ellen would be all right, and she assured me that she would wake up once Noah's effect wore off. She also said she probably wouldn't remember any of what happened. I shrugged my bag with mine and Ollie's stuff in it on my back, and stepped outside into the early evening sun. I expected to find a car in the driveway belonging to the trio, but Ellen's old Toyota Camry was the only one there.

"You guys didn't drive here?" I asked.

Maya answered for the group. "We don't exactly have cars in Arrortha. None of us knows how."

I looked at her to see if she was kidding, but it was pretty clear she wasn't. I didn't know how to drive, either; nobody had taught me, and there was no way Rose was going to let me learn in one of her cars.

"So, how did you get here?" I asked.

"What you guys call a train, a couple buses, and a lot of walking," Maya said.

"You said there actually *is* a portal that will take us to...?" I trailed off, unable to remember the name.

"Arrortha, and yes, I wasn't lying. It's in Denver."

"So we're flying there?"

"Ha!" Lucinda said sharply. "That's what they would want us to do. Get you trapped in a metal tube very high in the air.

Doesn't matter how strong you are, you're easy pickings up there. No, we're taking trains or buses. Anything that stays on the ground."

I didn't see how being stuck in a metal tube on the ground was much better, but I didn't push her any further.

Lucinda continued, "And before you ask, we don't use the same money in Arrortha, and we used most of the Earth dollars we had locating you, so if you wouldn't mind chipping into your own rescue fund, it would be greatly appreciated."

I was a fifteen-year-old kid; I didn't have money.

"Mom and Dad have a safe," Ollie said.

He was right, and I knew the code. I didn't have money, but Rose and Dane did.

Ollie and Maya followed me back into the house and to the master bedroom. Buried deep in the closet was a small safe that I had been given the combination to. Rose had made it very clear, both before and after telling me the code, that they "Knew exactly how much was in the safe," and that I was to only get into it in case of emergencies.

This counted as one, right?

I brought it out to the room, setting it on the bed. After pressing in the four-digit code, the door popped open. Expensive looking jewelry, coins, and computer hard drives sat neatly on top of stacks of paper. A blue, zipped shut bank bag was tucked into the corner of the safe. I pulled it out first, flipping it over to read the front. White letters spelled out "Capitol Pane Credit Union: A Glimpse into Your Financial Future." The bag unzipped at the top. I reached my hand in, pulling out a stack of bills. After counting them, it added up to just over three thousand dollars.

"Will that be enough to get all of us to Denver?" Maya asked.

I shrugged and nodded, rezipping the bag. "I think so."

Looking back into the safe, I spotted a pair of blue cards under a stack of gold rings. I pulled them out, reading the "Social Security" written in capital letters across the top. Rose and Dane must've been given a copy of mine and Ollie's social security cards. I put them in my pocket, not sure what I would need them for, but not wanting to leave them behind.

* * *

We met Vincent and Lucinda back in the driveway. Lucinda took the bag from me right away, stashing it under her arm while she grabbed three booklets from her cloak that were about the size and shape of a passport.

"What are those?" I asked.

She pulled one from the rest and handed it to me.

It was identical to a United States passport. A picture of Vincent, who stared blankly into the camera, sat on the bottom left corner of the open booklet.

"How did you get these?"

"They look real, don't they? Those took the greatest minds in Arrortha to make. That, and a couple of trips to Earth to find one of those picture-taking devices."

"A camera?"

"Yes! These passports got us here, and they'll get us back," she said, taking it back from me and storing them, and the cash, in her cloak. "Let's go catch a train."

She turned and started walking across the street. I was

impressed; she was heading in the direction of the station. The others turned to follow her.

"Are you really walking there?" I called after her.

"Unless you have a better idea," she said without turning back.

"Actually, I do," I said, pulling out my phone and opening the Uber app. I'd created an account a couple of weeks ago using a fake birthday. I didn't look eighteen by any means, but in limited use it hadn't been questioned. After a couple of clicks the app told me a SUV was on its way. The driver, Thomas, who looked too old in his picture to be driving himself, let alone anyone else, was about ten minutes away.

"A car will be here in ten minutes to pick us up," I said to the group, making its way back across the street.

"How did you do that?" Lucinda asked.

I held up my phone. "Earth technology."

"Nice. Now lose it," she said, knocking the phone out of my hand, sending it tumbling onto the concrete driveway below. I started to ask what was wrong with her when she held up her walking staff, the orb glowing bright blue. A quick flash escaped it, and a thick layer of ice appeared around my phone.

I looked wide-eyed at Lucinda, who smirked back at me.

"Like I said, child, you have a lot to learn."

Chapter Three

I was still fuming from my phone being encapsulated in ice when an expensive-looking Cadillac Escalade pulled up to the curb. Its windows were tinted, and I saw a reflection of myself instead of the driver. Soon the driver's window rolled down, revealing the head of an older man, his wispy gray hair combed neatly to one side. Freckles lined his cheeks, some hidden by the dimples on his smiling face. Thick sunglasses covered his face, but he removed them as he spoke.

"You must be Jaden," he said, tucking the glasses into the front pocket of his button-up shirt.

"Are you Thomas?"

"Oh, please, call me Tom. Tommy, if you prefer," he said with a wink. "Hop in. There's plenty of room for the five of ya!"

Lucinda and I made our way to the other side of the car. As we walked behind the back of the luxury SUV, a multitude of bumper stickers attached to the back window and trunk contrasted the black paint. Lines of stick figures danced around stickers of animals, political figures, and other quips. A giant Uber sticker headlined the window, hovering just above a green sticker with white lettering that read "Even my wrinkles have wrinkles."

The interior of the Escalade was just as nice as the exterior. Lucinda sat in the passenger seat next to Tom, who kept turning to face her and grinning. Maya sat in the middle row next to me, and Ollie and Vincent moved back to the third row. I wanted Ollie next to me, but he seemed comfortable with Vincent, as he was already talking his ear off about his Power Rangers collection. Vincent, to his credit, asked questions and let Ollie explain each figure and their abilities. I wondered if they had Power Rangers in Arrortha, or if Vincent was that good at making things up on the fly.

I looked out the window in silence for a couple of minutes.

Maya leaned over toward me. "What was it like?" she asked, her voice soft and friendly.

"What was what like?"

"Growing up on Earth, dude! What was it like?"

I shrugged. "I don't know. Normal, maybe."

"Even without your parents?"

I turned to look at her.

She drew back, her cheeks turning red under her tan skin. "I'm sorry, that came out wrong. I just meant without having your real parents here since... well, since your dad is... I'm sorry, that also came out wrong—"

I interrupted her. "Since my dad is...?"

"You'd have no way of knowing," she said, more to herself.

"Your dad was killed shortly after you were born. He died protecting you. I'm sorry."

He's dead? And he died... protecting me?

I sat back in my seat. My father did care for me, much more than I could've ever imagined. I thought I never knew him for other reasons, but I suppose that explained where he'd been my whole life. I looked down at the floor. I felt... guilty. Other weird feelings ran wild inside of me, but anger seemed to come out on top. I was angry at myself for assuming he had abandoned me, but I couldn't blame myself for the assumption, either. I grew up thinking no one wanted me. Everything this trio had told me went against that, and I was fighting it.

"I thought he abandoned me," I whispered.

"Abandon you? Jaden, he would never have. Neither would Queen Iris."

I must have given her a funny look, because she added, "Oh! Queen Iris is your mother. She's the best."

Voices up front distracted me from the conversation with Maya. I caught "beautiful hair," from Tom, who stared across the vehicle at Lucinda rather than the road in front of him. Lucinda gave no acknowledgment he existed, but that didn't deter Tom the Uber Driver.

Tom said, "And those gorgeous baby blues! Oh my, they could paint a picture in my soul."

Lucinda glared at him. "I'm going to freeze your soul if you don't—"

"Ah, Grandma, he's just trying to be nice!" I said, hanging my torso over the center console to be between them. "Excuse her, Tom. She gets angry in the evenings. We're going to her favorite pizza place on the edge of town, so she probably hasn't eaten all day to save room."

"It's no problem, son. How about some music? What are you kids into these days?" He looked down at his phone, which was Bluetoothed to his car.

"How about this?" he asked, clicking on a song. Lil Wayne's "A Milli" blasted through the Escalade, the bass rattling in the trunk.

"This was before I was born," I mumbled, sitting back in the middle row. Tom may not have known what year it was, but I had to give it to him, his music taste wasn't bad.

A minute later, and with Tom fully focused on the rush hour traffic, Lucinda turned around to face the back of the car.

"Open your hand," she said. I did, and in it she placed a slim metal ring. The outer rims were a polished graphite color, with the bulk of the ring a solid black. A lighter gray line snaked its way between the outer rims, separating the ring into distinct halves. I turned it over and over in my hand. With each flip, my hand tingled wherever it touched.

"What's this?" I asked her.

"It is the most powerful item in Arrortha," she said. "It belongs to a cursed immortal woman named Krera."

"Why is she cursed?"

"For things she did in her past. Things not known to anyone, even her."

I didn't understand this whole cursed immortal woman thing, or why I had her ring now, but Lucinda didn't let me dwell on it for long.

"For as long as I know, it's been handed down from ruler to

ruler. Whoever is leading Arrortha is wearing the ring, though less and less are respecting that...." She trailed off, before shaking her head and starting again. "It was handed down to me by my dad, and I gave it to your mother when I chose her to take power. She gave it back to me so I could give it to you to help you get back."

I kept inspecting it, asking, "So I will be the ruler if I put it on? Does it have magical powers?"

"Technically, yes, and it does multiple things. Most relevant to you will be its weapons, which we will expand on when we're out of this car."

Ruler? Weapons? All from a piece of jewelry?

"Maya, will you try to show him why his last name is 'Frost,' please? I'm going to keep an eye out for trouble," she said, turning to look out the front.

Maya explained, in under a minute, how powers worked in Arrortha. She said that when you reach twelve years old, you are given a choice to gain powers, like she did, or stay without them, like Vincent. Should you choose to receive a power, you went to see this immortal woman named Krera—whose ring I now had —and she would grant you one of six possible powers. Maya believed they were randomly assigned, but she wasn't sure.

"You've already seen what a Desolate can do," she said. "And I'm a Medela. The other four include Lapis, Crescere, Ferrum, and Glacies. Or stone, plant, iron, and ice, if you prefer English—"

I did, actually.

"—Lucinda is a Glacies, as your phone found out."

"So, I have the Desolate power, even though I've never been to Arrortha?" I asked.

"Technically, you have all of them."

"How's that possible?"

"Well, because you're cursed, too," she said, as if it was perfectly normal.

At times I've felt cursed, but to hear someone say I actually am pretty much blew my mind. "What do you mean, I'm cursed?"

"You were cursed when you were born in Arrortha, giving you every power, which is why you were sent here to Earth."

"I don't understand. Cursed by who?"

"Look, Jaden, I promise we will answer any questions you have, but they need to wait at least until we're on the train. We need to see what you know how to do now, so I'm sorry, but answers will have to wait. Put the ring on."

I was getting annoyed by the lack of answers. Still, I could feel the ring buzzing as it neared my finger. I slid it onto my right hand, the ring adjusting its size to fit my finger perfectly. An electrical shock, like I'd been struck by lightning, rocketed through the rest of my body as the ring settled. The shock faded to a small buzz before disappearing, but I felt connected to the ring in a way I couldn't explain. Light escaped the outer edges of it, moving slowly toward the middle of the ring. When it reached it, it exploded out of the centerline, covering the ceiling of Tom's Escalade in a dazzling shine. It soon faded, but the snaking line remained illuminated all-white.

"Well, that's certainly never happened before," Lucinda said, having seen the light show on the ceiling.

"Nobody like him has worn it," Vincent said from the back seat.

"Nobody like me?" I asked, facing him.

"Whoa!" Ollie said, a mesmerized look on his face. "How are you making your eyes do that? They're glowing!"

I looked at myself in the rearview mirror. Just like Ollie had said, both of my eyes sparkled, leaving a faint blue glow against the pale skin under them.

"Still not as bright as yours," Tom said, winking at Lucinda, who huffed back at him.

The orb on her lap shone brightly, but to her credit, she didn't freeze him.

"It's beautiful," Maya said, grabbing my hand.

Instinctively, I pulled it back and out of her grasp. I felt bad immediately and tried to make a joke of it, but nothing came to mind, so I just mumbled "Sorry."

She looked hurt, but quickly moved on to business. "Or not. Your dad was a Glacies, so that's what we think will be your strength. Hold out your hand. I promise I won't grab it," she winked at me from across the car.

I knew nothing about her, but still, she was pretty in the evening light. But if there was one thing I understood less than my own emotions, it was other people, especially girls. They are so complex, and after fifteen years, I was not remotely close to understanding them. I wondered if healers had some other power she wasn't telling me about, but I pushed the thought away and focused on what she was about to tell me. I held out my hand, palm up.

"This is going to sound crazy, but all you have to do is think about creating ice, and you can. Start with your fingertips and work your way to the whole hand."

I curled my ring and middle finger in, my hand taking the shape Spiderman does whenever he shoots a web.

"You don't have to do that," Maya said.

I said softly, "Okay," and straightened them back out.

I looked at my fingertips, concentrating on what she just said. I tried as hard as I could, praying this wasn't some cruel joke. The tips of my fingers tingled, but nothing appeared on them. I closed my eyes, took a deep breath, and focused as much as I could.

After a couple of seconds, Maya exclaimed, "There you go!"

I opened my eyes in disbelief. Ice crystals had formed on my hand, covering it. I looked back toward Ollie. His eyes were closed and his hand was out in front of him, no doubt attempting to do the same. He, unfortunately, wasn't having the luck I was.

The frost on my hand disappeared as I lost focus on it. It appeared to melt away, but once it was gone, my hand remained dry. I focused my attention on my fingers again, wanting to see the crystals form with my own eyes. After a couple seconds of trying, they appeared. I marveled at them, then thought about making them disappear. On command, they vanished.

"You can make it go away by thinking about it, too, as you've figured out," Maya said. "Keep practicing with it, but be careful. The powers are still cursed, and so are you. If you use them too much, you'll hurt yourself more than anyone else."

The white marble Union Train Station suddenly loomed outside my window. As we melted into the slow-moving traffic of

Columbus Circle, I feared I was starting to believe everything I'd been told today; maybe I wouldn't want to go back. Tom navigated around other parked cars to take a front row spot, much to the dismay of a red-and-gray taxi. We climbed out of the Escalade, joining the mess of others heading to the station. Tom left us with an "Enjoy your dinner," and a smile as he drove off, although I'm sure it was directed at Lucinda. Ollie held onto my wrist as we filed under massive arches and through glass doors that led into the station.

Chapter Four

The entryway to Union Station put us into a giant lobby. Polished floors led to stone walls, which opened into massive decorative arches with skylights, allowing ample natural light to fill the lobby. Historical stone statues were scattered above the tunnels that led to other areas of the station, and I felt they, too, just like the ones at school, stared at me.

The main lobby was filled with people arriving back home after a long day of work. Almost all the travelers looked the part: Their shoulders drooped, heads hung low, their bags, or briefcases nearing the floor as they walked. Most paid no attention to those around them, which was good for us. I'm sure our odd quintuplet normally would've drawn numerous looks, given the fact one of us had glowing eyes.

I did my best to avoid bumping into anyone as we weaved our way toward the ticket counter. Large crowds made me anxious, even more than I normally am. Just the thought of being surrounded by nothing but people is enough to make me shudder. So once we broke free of the exiting passengers and into the Amtrak portion of the station, I breathed a little easier. This area of the station was older and more commercial-looking. Fewer windows lined the upper walls, so most of the lighting came from the neon signs that advertised business and food stores.

Lucinda reached inside her cloak as we approached the ticket window. I blocked her path, grabbing the wrist that held the zipped-up bank bag in it.

"Let me do the talking. You haven't quite figured out Earthly manners yet," I said. I swear she growled, but she handed me a stack of cash and the passports. I stepped up to the counter, putting on my best *I know what I'm doing* grin.

Behind the glass window was a middle-aged woman with a nose piercing and a large wad of bubblegum in her mouth. She looked bored and did not return my smile.

"How are you today?" I asked.

She responded by blinking and blowing an enormous bubble.

"Okay. I need five tickets to Pittsburgh."

Without looking away, she started typing on the computer next to her while blowing another bubble. I examined the many posters on the glass while I waited.

"The next train isn't until tomorrow. But it's your lucky day, isn't it? The four oh-five train is still here."

The clock on the wall behind her showed it was well after six. "Why?"

"I don't know, kid. Something about rocks on track nineteen, but they're probably about cleared now. Do you want the tickets or not? I need to see IDs."

I did want the tickets. She gave me a weird look when I pulled the wad of cash and the trio's fake passports, along with mine and Ollie's social security cards. She gave them a half glance, more interested in watching me choose five one-hundred-dollar bills. As she slid everything across the counter, she asked, "You a trust-fund baby or something?"

I said, "Something like that," and grabbed the tickets.

It was a short walk through the rest of the station to find track nineteen. Like the ticket lady said, the 4:05 train to Pittsburgh sat darkened, waiting for the track to be cleared. A station worker told us it would still be at least half an hour before it would depart, so we decided to grab some dinner at the McDonald's inside the station.

We ordered and found a table near the front. I picked at the burger in front of me, the thoughts about my newfound powers, the ring I now wore, and how my real mom who cared about me was alive and well in some different realm taking precedence over eating.

Across the table, Vincent, Maya, and Lucinda discussed travel plans while looking at a large unfolded map of the United States they had picked up at an information kiosk. I heard names of cities in the USA, each bringing up arguments from someone in the group about why we should avoid or go through them.

I tuned them out and looked back toward the travelers inside the station. There were far fewer this deep into the station, so I could look closer at each one. A woman bent over a stroller, shaking a doll in an attempt to console her baby. Farther away, a group of college students huddled around a TV outside a pizza shop, but I couldn't tell what they were watching. A bald man walked by the window right in front of me. He wore a large jacket that went down to his knees, covering up the top half of his far too-tight pants. A belt was fastened around the outside of the jacket, making him walk awkwardly. I followed him with my eyes until another traveler stole them: Noah walked out of the Amtrak ticket station, scanning everyone.

I ducked a little lower, hoping a glare from outside would make seeing us through the window difficult. He must have missed us, because he turned and walked toward the other end of the station.

I looked away from the window. Maya held up her burger in front of her face. It looked sad as it hung from her fingers. Eventually, the bread ripped, and the sandwich tumbled onto the table below.

"Do you guys eat this stuff?" she asked.

"It's not all that bad. Did you see Noah?"

"Where?" Lucinda asked, the orb on her staff glowing.

"In the station," I said, pointing out of the restaurant. "He went toward the other end."

"I doubt he's alone. We should get on the train," she said. Lucinda directed her attention toward Maya and Vincent. "You two make sure nobody is waiting for us. We will follow you when it's clear."

We made a quick plan for Maya to come get us when they made sure we could get to the train without trouble. Then Maya and Vincent stood and left, heading for the gate.

I decided to keep watching the station to see if Noah came back. I hoped he didn't; one fight where he almost killed me was enough.

As Maya and Vincent passed through the gate, a reflection of light caught my eye. A woman stood against a wall about thirty feet away from the gate, wearing the same weird clothing as the man I'd seen. She looked like she had stuck her face in a bucket of mixed-up makeup. I've never worn makeup, but I think even I could've done better. Something slender and silver hung below her long coat, reflecting the light from a nearby shop sign as it dangled. As I watched, she refastened her belt a little higher, the silver item disappearing underneath her coat. The woman looked away from the gate, scanned the rest of the station, then walked off in the direction Noah had gone.

I got an uneasy feeling in my stomach as I watched her go. "You don't think he's alone?" I asked Lucinda, who still looked confident, but she too watched those around us a little closer.

"We shouldn't go into detail with the little one around, but I will say a certain someone back home would prefer it if you didn't make it back to Arrortha," she said.

"I'm almost eleven!" Ollie said back to her.

"And you're already so big and strong!" she said, smiling at him. To me, she said, "He will have help."

I turned back toward the station, but the woman was gone. I was beginning to get nervous.

Maya walked back through the gate a couple of minutes after the woman disappeared. There were only a handful of people on the train, and we shouldn't have any trouble getting on it, she told us. We threw away our trash and left the McDonald's, Ollie clinging to my side. I wrapped my arm around him, resting my hand on his shoulder.

As we readied our tickets, a familiar voice called out my name. Noah walked toward us, the oddly dressed man and woman on one side of him. A massive dude with a full lumberjack beard, dressed like the other two, walked on Noah's other side. Lucinda grabbed Ollie's and my tickets and threw them at the ticket-taker while ushering us through the gate.

"He doesn't care about all the people around. He will try to kill you right here," she said.

Once through the gate, a concrete platform split into pathways that walked alongside the different numbered tracks. Track nineteen shared a runway with track twenty, which was up against the outside of the station.

Vincent waited for us down the runway. I made it about halfway down the length of it when Noah stepped through the gate, the other three following close behind him.

"Jaden!" Noah yelled out, his voice echoing off the trains and concrete pillars. "You can't keep running from me."

He was right, mainly because I was at the end of the runway. I pulled Ollie behind me, putting myself between him and Noah's ugly friends, who were now halfway down the runway, with Noah right behind them. Vincent and Maya stepped by my side. Lucinda and Ollie behind me.

I was terrified now.

Noah's group stopped, sizing us up.

I used the brief pause to turn to Lucinda. "Will you get him to safety?" I asked her. If I was going to die here, hopefully Ollie could get away.

"Way ahead of you," she said, shooting out her hand to the track on her right. Ice shot out of it in streams, forming a bridge that stretched all the way to the runway on the other side. I handed her my bag and she grabbed Ollie, who almost ripped off a piece of my sweatshirt before he let go. He kicked and cried out as she dragged him across the bridge. I hated leaving him, but I knew whatever was about to happen on this runway was going to be much worse.

Lucinda waved her hand at the bridge once she was on the other side. Just as quickly as it formed, the bridge disappeared entirely, leaving nothing but a few small puddles of water on the tracks.

I forced myself to focus back on the danger in front of me. If I'd thought the situation was bad before, it had gotten much worse. Glistening swords, with blades at least a foot long, appeared in the hands of the trio. The belts they had worn now lay on the concrete floor; no doubt they had kept the swords hidden.

Vincent pulled out his necklace and grabbed the pendant from it. It formed into his double-sided ax, which he held at the ready. Maya revealed her pendant, but from where I was, it just looked like a stick. As she removed it, the stick grew until it was almost as tall as she was. It culminated at the top into a sharp tip made of the same rock-like material as the blade of Vincent's ax.

I swiftly realized I was the only person in this fight without a weapon. Across the track, Lucinda yelled at me as if she could read my mind. At this point, she might've been able to.

"Use the ring!" she said. "Tell the ring what you want. It is at your command!"

There is no way this ring can make a weapon, I thought. But as I did so, the ring glowed and vibrated on my finger. A pulse, like I'd just smacked my elbow on a table, escaped from my finger, shooting up my arm, into my chest and neck, and into my head. It's hard to describe, but I felt connected to the ring, like it would try its best to do whatever I asked of it. Crazy things had been happening all day today, so I gave it a shot. I made sure to only talk to the ring in my mind. Just in case it didn't work, I didn't want to look like an idiot talking to a piece of jewelry before I got gutted.

I had no experience with this type of thing. The sword fighting part, that is; I talked to myself all the time. Still, I told the ring to make the coolest weapon I could think of: dual swords. The ring vibrated in response.

My hands curled around the grips of a sword as they manifested out of thin air. I watched as black-and-silver blades grew from their own black hilt, each growing to almost two feet long before coming to a hooked end, like an old pirate sword. White shards of ice shot down the length of both swords, reaching the tip before disappearing and restarting from the bottom. They felt balanced and dangerous in my hands; they were the sickest things I'd ever seen in my life. There was only one problem: I had no idea how to use them, and they weren't going to give me time to learn.

The lumberjack raised his sword, stabbing it down toward the concrete. I expected it to snap in half between the guy's massive forearms and the hard floor, but instead it sliced into the concrete like it was made of foam. A wave of energy ran down the length of the blade, creating a crater that stretched toward us. A crack erupted from the crater, racing its way toward Vincent, who leaped off the platform and onto the track to avoid it. Lumberjack jumped off to meet him, and I was glad it wasn't me who had to try to fight that guy.

The baldheaded man and the woman with the horrific makeup charged forward next, their swords menacing. Beside me, Maya feigned a throw with her spear, causing the bald guy to drop into a roll to avoid the potential danger. The woman never broke stride and jumped into the air, swinging with both arms as she landed. Maya ducked out of the way as the sword pummeled into the ground where she had been. She countered with her spear, but it deflected harmlessly away with a metallic clank. I could hear more sounds of metal colliding from the track below me, but baldy appeared in front of me before I could see how Vincent was doing.

He swung down with his sword. With a cry, I brought mine to my left side. His weapon caught both of mine flush, sending white-hot sparks rocketing from where the three met. The force of his swing knocked me off balance, almost spinning me around. Wide-eyed, I fell to my back as a second swing sliced the air above me. He slammed his sword into the ground, but I'd already rolled away and scrambled to my feet, my swords in the shape of an X in front of me.

What did I get myself into?

Bald-head sneered as he approached me a second time. He swung again, but this time I was ready. I deflected it easily, sending his sword back the way it had come. He used this momentum to spin around and swing backhanded. The sixth sense that aided me in fights my whole life worked overtime now. I jumped over the sword, which swung by my ankles, then parried a third attack aimed for my chest, which got an audible, frustrated grunt from the guy.

I either avoided or deflected every attack he tried against me. My sixth sense seemed to transfer to melee weapons, as it took control, moving my body to where it needed to be. But I was tiring.

I struggled to catch my breath as I dodged the third move in a combo of attacks he tried.

"Just die already!" he yelled at me.

"Call it a tie?" I heaved back.

We stared at each other, panting. I tried my best to avoid passing out from exhaustion. Movement to my left stole his attention. I was too tired to look.

"Yo, Frosty, play offense!" Vincent yelled.

How long have you been watching and not helping me? "I don't know how," I said, sure I was about to throw up.

The man in front of me readied his sword again.

"Oh, come on," I muttered, struggling to stand straight.

He started toward me, but stopped, bringing his hand up like he was trying to make something levitate. I almost pretended like he was choking me out using the force, like they did in Star Wars, but I couldn't waste the energy. He raised his hand until it was shoulder level, his arm shaking like doing this was taking a lot of effort.

Without warning, he flung his hand across his body. A voice called, "Look out!" but it was too late. An object slammed into me from my left. A physical pain worse than I'd ever felt before flooded my side as the object dug into my abdomen between my ribs and hip, cutting deeper until it sent me tumbling to the concrete below, no longer able to stand. I gasped for air, the world spinning around me, as the thing reached its resting place deep in my side. The jolt from the landing loosened the object, and it fell out onto the floor beside me.

It looked like a sizable chunk of concrete, though it was now bright red and shiny. I had no idea where it had come from, or who had thrown it that hard. Had the bald guy controlled it with his hand? My head ached, and I fought to stay conscious. I coughed, which hurt more than you could possibly imagine. A warm, metallic liquid filled my mouth. I knew the taste of blood, and I spit it onto the ground next to me. I coughed again, and more blood filled my mouth from the back of my throat. *That can't be good.*

A shadow loomed over me. Someone rolled me onto my back, the pain bringing fresh tears. The tip of a sword poked into my chest right above my heart, the hilt of which was gripped firmly by the bald-headed guy, who appeared to have no intention of rushing my death. He taunted me as the blade pierced my skin, and a new pain formed in my chest. I prepared myself for my last moments on Earth to be rather unpleasant.

Suddenly, the flat black surface of Vincent's ax flew through the air, catching him square in the nose. An audible crunch echoed on the platform as he flew backward, landing hard on the ground before lying still.

Maya arrived at my side, sliding on her knees. She bumped into my side, causing me to howl in pain.

"My bad!" she exclaimed as she gently touched the wound.

The cooling sensation I felt earlier returned. Blood in my mouth dried, leaving nothing but the metallic aftertaste. The pain softened a little, but it was nowhere close to gone when she removed her hand.

"More, please," I begged.

She grabbed at her own side, wincing. "I can't."

The PA system in the station chimed above us. "First call for the delayed four oh five train to Pittsburgh," an automated voice called out.

Vincent helped me sit up. A sharp pain still shot through my left side, but after a few breaths it was manageable.

"What happened to the other two?" I asked.

47

"Don't worry about them," he replied, but offered nothing more.

I leaned forward to stand, slowly, when I heard a child's scream.

Ollie! I climbed to my feet; the pain threatened to send me right back to the floor. Maya yelped next to me as she stood before she did fall again. Vincent looked frustrated with her, but huddled in close to her and spoke softly. Maya nodded as if answering a question.

"Go help Lucinda," Vincent told me. "I'll stay here with her."

"No, I'm f—" she started, but she couldn't complete the sentence without doubling over.

I felt bad, but didn't understand what had happened to her. A second scream ripped me from my thoughts and I staggered down the runway in search of my brother.

I spotted him on the platform near the gate. He clutched my bag, cowering in the corner next to a giant sheet of ice that blocked the doorway back to the station. Noah swung his dagger wildly in front of him, Lucinda meeting each strike with her staff. The sound of each impact blasted across the runway as clouds of white ice exploded from the staff each time Noah struck it with the knife.

My body protested with every step. Still, I pushed forward, sweat droplets falling down my face from the exertion.

The tide of the fight in front of me was turning. Noah appeared to be far less experienced, but he was significantly younger, and while Lucinda still deflected his attacks, her reactions were slowing. When Noah's dagger narrowly missed her face, I did the only thing I could think of from how far away I was: I yelled his name and threw a sword.

Now, I'd like to tell you it arced through the air perfectly and implanted itself into Noah's chest, but that would be a lie. No, it made it maybe forty feet before it landed and skidded toward him. Before you laugh, know this: It worked. As he turned to face me and the sliding sword, Lucinda raised her arms, surrounding herself and Ollie in a cocoon of ice.

The sword came to a rest underneath Noah's foot. He picked it up, admiring the shards of ice running the length of the blade.

He started walking toward me as he spoke. "The Queen's people protecting you, your eyes are now glowing, and you've even got Krera's ring. You *are* Maledictus, aren't you?"

I shrugged. "Honestly, I'm trying to figure it all out myself."

"Don't bother. You won't live long enough."

I was really starting to not like this guy. We stood ten feet apart, one of my swords in my hand, the other in his. Union Station saw thousands of people a day, but surely the young man in a black flight jacket and the sweaty kid with a sliced up hoodie, who were about to duke it out medieval style, were by far the most interesting.

Vincent's comment came back to me. How *do* I play offense? I figured I would at least swing my sword this time.

And that's exactly what I did. As he stepped closer, I swung with both hands, the blade slicing through the air. Noah ducked out of the way and stabbed his sword straight forward, but I saw it coming and jumped to the side as it passed by. He recovered quickly, attacking from my left. I blocked his blade with mine and tried to twist, hoping it might dislodge the weapon from his hand, but the metal scraped and separated. He swung again, this time from straight overhead. I raised up to block it, but his strength brought both swords toward my face. The tip of his blade got so close to my nose I went cross-eyed looking at it. I let his sword take mine all the way down, the momentum preventing him from stabbing into my gut. He swung at my neck, the edge of the blade parallel to the ground, but I limboed under it as it passed inches above my nose.

Noah took a step back, twirling the sword in his hand.

A plan formed in my mind. I let go of the sword with my right hand, letting it dangle to my side. I focused on forming ice like I did in the car, and instantly my fingertips frosted over. I wanted him to think I could do more than just freeze my hand. He lunged forward, swinging at my exposed side, just as I wanted. I shot my left arm across my body, my sword meeting his. The force of the block knocked him off balance and pivoted me on my right leg. I kicked him square in the chest with my left leg, knocking him onto his back.

My side throbbed, but I used the kick to close the distance between us. He got to his feet as I swung my sword. He tried to block it, but the timing and force behind my attack forced him to deflect my blade into his thigh, where it sliced through his jeans and into his leg. He yelled some choice words about my mother and swung madly with his sword. As if I'd been doing this all my life, I waited until the last possible moment to jump backward. I used my sword to propel his past me, and with his blade no longer a threat, I lunged forward, driving forward and up. The blade sank deep into his midsection.

Surprise filled his face as he stared down at it before looking up at me. A pained groan escaped his lips, and he fell backward onto the concrete platform, his dagger falling from a holster on his ankle and clattering to the floor. He let out a last breath before his eyes slowly closed, and he lay motionless.

My hand shook as I removed my sword. The adrenaline from the fight was draining, and the realization of what had happened set in.

Vincent and Maya walked up. Maya looked better than before, but still used Vincent to steady her.

"I… I didn't mean to—" I whispered, my voice trembling.

"Relax, you did what you had to do," Vincent said, a proud look on his face. He bent down to pick up the dagger. "Here, this belongs to you now."

The last thing I wanted was a souvenir from the fight, but Vincent insisted I take it. "Noah won't be the last to come after you, and you might not always have the ring."

I tried to hide my shaking hands as I took the dagger, flipping it over on my palm. The entire weapon was made of silver metal, with matching color tape wrapped around the base for grip. The figure of a snake had been carved into the blade, the tail starting at the tip and wrapping around until it reached its head, which made its way up to the end of the handle. The scales of the serpent flapped open with movement of the dagger, which I imagine made removing the blade very unpleasant.

The PA system rang out again, announcing the final call for the delayed 4:05 train. I hid the dagger and my sword behind my back as a couple of passengers poked their heads out of the train, no doubt wondering what all the commotion had been earlier. Noah's body was hidden behind us, and Vincent or Maya had moved the bald guy from the middle of the runway, making things look as normal as they possibly could. They stared at us for a few seconds before dipping back into the train.

Lucinda, with Ollie in tow, came striding toward us from the gate, their cocoon of ice completely gone. When he saw me, he let go of Lucinda's hand and bolted to me. I told the ring to remove the swords I still had, and on command, they disappeared.

A fire shot through my left side as Ollie wrapped me tight into a hug, but I didn't care. He was telling me all about what had happened as we walked to the train, leaving Noah where he was. Lucinda assured me that he wasn't from Earth, so it didn't matter. Still, it felt wrong.

We boarded the train and found our seats. Our car was completely empty outside of us, so we spread out. Ollie took the seat next to me, using a sweatshirt out of my bag as a pillow to lean against my shoulder. I watched the city race by in the dim light, more than happy to be leaving the station and DC behind.

Chapter Five

The train rattled on as darkness overtook the landscapes outside my window. After leaving the station, the conductor had announced we should all get comfortable, as we had "just under eight hours to spend together." Hours later, my nerves had just started to relax.

I stared out the window for most of the trip. The bustling evening rush in the city thinned out until we traveled through small towns and darkened fields. Ollie had fallen asleep some time ago, his head moving up and down my arm with each rhythmic breath. Through the dimmed cabin, I could see Vincent a couple of rows ahead of me, on the other side of the aisle. Now and then I could hear a soft snore over the clacking of the train as he slept, too.

Sleep was one of those luxuries I was not likely to get tonight. My mind raced far too fast to slow it down, so I let it run wild. It ventured through the day's events, from my classes with Barrett (which was somehow the least eventful thing that happened), all the way to winning my first sword fight. Vincent had removed Noah's scabbard and attached it to my leg on the train, and its hilt dug into my lower leg as I recalled the multiple times it narrowly missed my face.

Was this what my new life was going to be like?

A rustle of clothing drew me away from my thoughts. Maya sat down next to Ollie, who stirred only enough to adjust the sweatshirt against my arm. She had changed since getting on the train, now wearing an olive-green windbreaker and a pair of ripped jeans. She sat watching Ollie for a moment before looking at me, studying my face; I did my best to avoid eye contact and looked around the cabin of the train.

"Your eyes are kinda creepy in the dark," she said softly, as if not to wake Ollie.

I stopped looking around, instead looking straight down. "I can just keep them shut."

"No, then I can't see them." When the only answer I could muster was "Um," she laughed and changed topics. "How's your side?"

Truthfully, it hurt with every movement. So naturally, I told her it was fine. "What happened to yours?" I blurted out before she could respond.

She put her hand on her side as she spoke. "When I, or anyone with the Medela power, heals someone, that injury is transferred. It limits a healer's ability, which is why we can only do so much at one time with serious injuries. When the pain in your side was easing, the cut was actually healing, but it was causing the wound to happen to me. I wasn't thinking, and I took too much. But we heal quicker from inherited injuries, so the pain is almost gone. Plus, it helped you kill Noah, so I guess it was worth it."

"I guess so," I said.

"Speaking of which, you have that dagger now, right? Let me see it. I want to show you something."

I pulled it out of my leg holster and gave it to her. She inspected it in the dim light, getting real close to the blade to look at the scales that wrapped around it.

"I want you to heal me," she said. She drug the tip of the blade across her palm, leaving a cut. Blood bubbled around it, and she held her hand out to me.

I stared at it, unsure what to do. She'd already healed me twice, both times touching the injury itself. Hesitantly, I placed my hand on hers.

"Now what?" I asked.

"Now heal me. Just try it."

I brought my attention to where our hands met and did my best to heal her and discover how this magical power worked. I concentrated and felt... nothing. Trying again, I felt a small twinge in my hand. I removed it from hers, but the blood, and her cut, remained. It might've been smaller, but not enough to make a difference.

This was stupid. I pulled my hand away in frustration, wiping her blood on my pants and turning to look out the window. How fitting would it be for me to be cursed, have all these powers, and then not know how to use any of them?

"It's all right, Jaden. When you're first learning to heal, it's easier to learn on people you care about. It's how I learned," Maya said.

I turned sharply, Ollie moaning in protest. "Why are you doing this?" I asked, the words harsher than I wanted.

"Doing what?" Maya asked.

"Protecting me. Healing me. Attempting to teach me how to not be useless. Why are you doing any of this, and why won't you tell me anything? You said you would on the train, but nobody has."

"You killed Noah by yourself, while injured, with no training. That doesn't seem useless to me. And I am going to tell you." After a pause, she continued. "Look, it's my job to teach you these things and get you back safely, but it'll be easier to do it if you trust me."

There they were. My two least favorite words. *Trust me.* I've been let down before, and I didn't trust anyone. Sometimes not even myself. I tried not to show any expression, but inside I was hurting, frustrated, and annoyed. Not so much with her, but with myself. I berated myself as I simmered in the darkness.

Why do you think you don't let people get close, Jaden? You've avoided it for three years.

My left hand rose to my right forearm, probing the sweatshirt and feeling for the bump from a scar there. The night I'd been dumped off back at the Alvarez house, I took my anger out on the glassware in the dining room, throwing dishes and glasses at any wall I could find. A shard had ricocheted off one of the walls and sliced my arm open. I didn't even notice it until Mr. Alvarez discovered it, wrapping me tight as I sobbed into his arms.

The first girl that's willing to talk to you, and you let her in like she's the Queen of England. She doesn't care about you, she's just doing her job.

I closed my eyes, not knowing whether to cry or punch the train window, but I also didn't know why I felt this way. It was like a battle inside me for the next few minutes. Most of me wanted Maya away from me and out of my life. But a small part didn't want her to leave, begging for someone to cling to, to understand what I'd faced today. Someone other than Ollie. Don't get me wrong, he's my brother, and I love him, but he's only ten.

She sat quietly until I was ready to talk again. Eventually, the small piece of me won out enough to not tell her to get lost, but it told me to be careful.

"Noah called me a name. Mal-a-something."

"Maledictus. It means 'The Cursed One' in Latin."

"Okay, but why Latin? Nobody uses it anymore."

"*Linguae ne moriantur,*" she said. "You're going to have to learn it. English is used in Arrortha, but Latin is the main language."

Great, more school. "What does this place look like?"

"Oh, it's wonderful. Well, of course, there's the magic which structures our lives differently from what you've grown up with. You'll get used to it, with who your mother is and all. Unfortunately, that makes it more dangerous, especially for you." She cocked her head, as if she was thinking about what else to tell me. "But nature-wise, you can't find anything as beautiful on this side of the portal."

"Why is it more dangerous?"

"I've been told it wasn't always how it is now. At least not until *you* were born and cursed."

"So, I made it more dangerous... by... existing?"

"Pretty much."

My head hurt, but she continued. "It's not your fault, but it does have everything to do with you."

"How?" I asked, still baffled how a kid who didn't even know this place existed was responsible for *anything* that happened there.

"Lucinda used to be the Queen of Highmoore, which is the biggest and most powerful kingdom in Arrortha. Because of this, she was considered the Queen of Arrortha, depending on who you asked. Like any ruler, especially here, I've noticed, she wasn't liked by everyone; she can tell you about it later. Long story short, Lucinda has no relatives, so she had to choose who to take power next, and had it narrowed down to two candidates. One was your mother; the other was a guy named Ian Walker. Everyone expected her to choose him, to keep a Glacies in charge, and keep Highmoore as it is. As you can probably guess, she didn't. She chose your mom—"

"And Ian took it the wrong way," I guessed.

"Biggest understatement in Arrorthian history," she scoffed. "He tried to kill your mother out of spite. When your dad got in the way, well… Ian killed him. You were only a couple days old, but you were now next in line, so you were a threat, too. He couldn't get to you, so he cursed you, and escaped somewhere in Arrortha for the last fifteen years. He's been building a following, so Queen Iris sent us to bring you back. We assumed he was sending people to look for you, too, and now we know for sure he is."

"So this Ian guy is the reason I'm cursed?"

She nodded. "And because he cursed himself too, he's also the reason it's more dangerous for you."

58

"How?"

"Power and fear have always decided who rules in Arrortha. It's how our leaders get 'chosen,' even Lucinda."

"She was feared?"

Maya nodded. "People used to call her the 'Ice Witch.' A lot still do. You did not want to be on her bad side. But as time went on, she started to change. People say it was all a show to be remembered more favorably, but then she stepped down and chose your mother. Queen Iris has a… *different* opinion on how Arrortha should be led. She's more of a believer in everyone, and that helping everyone, not just those who can help her, will create a better place. I think it's the Medela inside of her."

"And now she has a cursed son to show for it?"

"That, and an enemy with the same curse trying to restore Highmoore to what it used to be. Queen Iris has gotten a lot of people to agree with her, but there are still so many that don't. As for you, outside of having all the powers, we don't know what else you're cursed with, so just, you know, be careful."

"Okay."

We sat quietly in the dim cabin as the lights of a small town twinkled in the distance beyond the dark fields.

"So has Arrortha always existed?" I asked.

Maya took a couple of seconds before replying. "Good question," she said. "We think so, but Krera might be the only one who knows that, and she isn't the most open about her past. We're taught she was cursed during a massive war, one that she was the only survivor of."

"How did she survive it?"

"You can ask her if you get the chance. She grants us powers when we're twelve. Outside of that, she wants nothing to do with us."

"How is she able to give us powers?" I asked.

She smiled at me through the low light. "There is so much I wish I knew. And believe me, I asked Krera herself these same questions when I went to get my power, but she ignored all of them." She paused, her gaze moving to Ollie, who slept unbothered despite the talking. Her face softened as she watched the sleeping boy. "You'll both fit in well there," she said. She looked back up at me. "Especially you, Maledictus. You're going to be a celebrity."

That was pretty much the last thing I wanted to hear. "That's great."

"You've got to get there in one piece first, though, Frosty. Get some sleep," she said, standing up. "Might be a long couple of days, and you had an interesting day today."

"One last question," I said before she could walk away. "How do I know how to fight? I've felt like I've had a sixth sense my whole life, but it felt like it came alive today."

"You can thank your dad for that. He was Glacies, too, so it's your best ability. Fighting will come naturally to you. Glacies are the greatest warriors in Arrortha, though they're vastly outnumbered by the other powers. Anyway, that sixth sense you're referring to is part of you and your curse. You're able to do a lot of things you don't know you can. But that'll start tomorrow, Jaden. Try to sleep now." She turned with a friendly smile and went back to her seat.

I watched her as she walked away. Despite my outburst earlier, I liked her, and that terrified me. I leaned back in my seat. A flare of pain shot up my side from the contact, but at least it took my mind off her. I willed myself to think about literally anything else as I settled in for the rest of the ride, knowing sleep would not come easy.

Chapter Six

I f you've never tried yawning with a massive cut on your side, I would *not* recommend the experience. I stared out the window, hoping to fall asleep, but as each yawn increased the intensity of the pain, I gave up and stared into the dark as the train rattled on.

Long after Maya had left, Lucinda took the seat next to me. She asked questions about the fight, which I answered, but I was more interested in what she did. I thanked her for protecting Ollie, then asked her how she made the large wall of ice.

"Practice, experience, and situation. It is nearly impossible to master the power, but you can control it, probably better than I can," she added. "But to do that, you'll need to learn the basics. For now, just practice freezing and unfreezing your hand."

I tried it a few times, each time forming small ice crystals that sat on my palm, then disappearing whenever I wanted them to. Lucinda gave me a nod, and as she stood to return to her seat, told me to keep practicing whenever I could.

Well into the early morning hours, the conductor came back on the intercom, announcing our arrival into Pittsburgh. Ollie stirred with the sound, and after a gentle nudge from me, he awakened fully. He yawned, forcing me to stifle my own as the train came to a rest in the station.

We exited the train with the few other passengers into a well-lit lobby that was nearly empty. A giant digital board hung from the center of the lobby, displaying train times and advertisements, along with a scrolling clock that read 2:38 a.m. We continued through the lobby and the waiting area of the station, until we were alone in the business section, walking past rows of darkened shops and food stores, none daring to be open at this hour.

"I overheard your conversation with Lucinda," Vincent said as we walked. "That power stuff is important, but your fighting skills are going to be your most important asset. You might want to learn some offense." I glanced at him. "Right now, you're annoyingly hard to kill, but you're not dangerous."

"Some might argue differently," I snapped back.

"He didn't know what he was doing. Besides, you may not always be prepared."

Then, like a blur, he spun, wielding a knife I didn't know he had. The blade ended up by my throat, the tip just inches away. "What do you do now?" he asked.

Without thinking, I whipped my left hand out, grabbed the wrist that held the knife, and pushed it up and away from me. With his wrist still in my grasp, I sidestepped to avoid the blade and swung my free hand, connecting with the inside of his elbow. His hand opened, and I caught the knife as it fell, holding it close to his throat like he'd done to me.

He smiled at me from the end of the blade.

"Boys!" Lucinda scolded. "Can you not kill each other before we get home?"

"Relax, Luce. He's better than he knows," Vincent said, still smiling.

I dropped the knife and let it clatter to the floor, turned, and kept walking toward the front doors.

As we continued in silence, I practiced controlling my Glacies power. I froze my hand and unfroze it, each time increasing the amount. By the time we reached the front of the station, I could freeze my entire hand and effortlessly remove it on command. Eventually, a swirling ball of ice, which danced in circles in the palm of my hand, formed. It became the size of an orange before it stopped growing and floated an inch above my skin. It looked like a boiling snowball.

"That's usually the last thing you learn," Lucinda said, pointing to my hand. "Put it away before someone sees."

The cooling night air greeted us as we left the building and entered a courtyard just outside the station. Bricks were laid in a circular pattern, meeting in the middle. Multiple archways made up the entrances, each one rising high into the ceiling. Designs carved into each corner pillar ended at a woman's head with the name of a major US city underneath. A brick ramp across the courtyard continued down into the street, where the sound of sirens echoed softly over the sleeping city.

Another sound echoed throughout the courtyard, stopping us in our tracks. A pulsing, metallic growl bounced off the stone walls, creating a reverb that surrounded us. It sounded deep and robotic, so I was shocked when a snake slithered into the open.

"Did that thing just growl?" I asked Maya, who stood next to me.

"Yes."

"They can do that?"

"I don't know. You grew up here, not me, but I'm guessing that's not a normal snake," she said.

"Why would it be? Nothing has been normal since you guys got here," I muttered as it swayed nearer.

Maya was right. As the animal entered the courtyard, it raised its head and balanced on the back half of its body, unveiling a hood around its neck. I'd seen pictures of a cobra before, and it was obvious that was what I was looking at.

Except this one was massive. It was standing almost six feet tall, tall enough that it was eye level with me, and as thick around as Ollie, its beady yellow eyes contrasting with its striped brown body. Behind it, a man stood between pillars, staring directly at me. Between the lighting and the cobra, I didn't get a good look at him before he turned and disappeared into the night.

Prove yourself, Maledictus, said a voice.

I looked at the others to see if they had heard the voice too, but their attention was fixated on the serpent. For the sake of not sounding crazy, I kept it to myself.

Vincent's ax appeared beside me. He sprinted away from us, drawing the beast's attention, which opened its mouth. The metallic growl rose in decibels, now booming in the courtyard. A crackling white ball of electricity grew in its mouth, swelling until it filled the space. Vincent brought his ax in front of him, ready to defend.

He braced for impact as the reptile spit the ball at him. The orb of energy impacted his ax in a dazzling display of blue and white. Electricity exploded, the sound like a lightning bolt in the middle of a thunderstorm. The ax went flying, as did Vincent, who hit the ground hard.

I made a mental note to avoid the exploding white balls as I ran toward Vincent, yelling to draw attention away from him. I didn't care much for the guy, but I wasn't going to let this monster get a free shot at him. The growl escalated, and through a quick glance, I could see I had the snake's undivided attention as it turned to track me. It sent an electric ball my way, and I flattened myself against the floor. The bricks did not provide the soft landing I was hoping for, and my ribs voiced their displeasure. The ball sailed over my head, out of the courtyard and into the city beyond.

I rose and kept sprinting, racing past Vincent, who was slowly getting to his feet. Another ball shot my way, and I ducked just in time as it darted past my ear with a buzzing sound. The ball exploded the pillar behind me, blasting off the nameplate that read "New York." It showered me with rock fragments, each one stinging my skin.

"Give me something!" I shouted at the ring.

On command, a short-handled sickle appeared in each hand, made of the same material and design the swords had been made of, but one sickle was the same black color, while the other was white. I didn't have time to admire them before the cobra loaded another electric ball.

"Keep its attention!" Maya yelled at me from across the courtyard.

That would be easy.

A third white ball launched my way. I prepared to duck, but the reptile had learned, aiming lower, placing the ball's trajectory right at my feet. I realized at the last minute and tried to dive to the side, but I didn't make it far enough. The electricity exploded, sending shocks up my legs. I landed flat on my stomach, my side flaring in pain. I fought the electricity for control of my body as the aftershocks sent ripples throughout it. I tried to stand, but my legs felt like jelly, the muscles twitching with minds of their own, each working against one another with every step.

I could hear another ball charging as the snake closed in for the kill. I turned my body to face it, bringing the sickles in front of me in a crossing pattern, hoping I could deflect the ball enough to where I could survive however far it threw me.

The cobra glowered at me through the sickles with its yellow eyes, the white ball in its mouth nearing full size. I stood as tall as my shaky legs would allow. The metallic growl reached a fever pitch, swelling inside the courtyard.

Suddenly, Maya's spear stabbed through the animal from behind, the tip abruptly glistening with black blood. The growl turned into a pained hiss as it shook violently, trying to free its body from the impalement. Maya held firm, and the shaking soon stopped as it went limp on the spear like a fresh, unappetizing kabob.

After a few seconds, it started shaking again, though much less forcefully. As it shook, it disappeared, until all that remained was the old skin that is left when a snake sheds. Maya looked disgusted as she peeled it off her spear and threw it on the ground.

The last of the hissing faded, letting the quiet ambiance of the city take its place. Lucinda and Ollie helped steady Vincent, so I teetered to Maya.

"Not normal," I said.

She half-smiled, but said nothing, instead looking at Vincent with a look of concern.

"Electricity. He probably hurts all over but should be fine," I said.

"Did you get hit?"

"Yeah. My legs are twitchy, but I'm sure it'll go away."

We moved toward the other three, where Vincent stood now. His short hair looked frazzled, but otherwise he showed no major effects from the fight.

Minutes later, we were headed down the ramp to the street. Vincent wobbled slightly as he walked, but insisted he didn't need any help, getting mad when Maya tried to steady him. We put our weapons away and did our best to look like normal travelers, though there was nobody on the streets this time of night.

We rounded the corner at the bottom of the ramp, crossing the intersection, where the bus station sat catty-corner.

The bus station, or Grant Street Transportation Center, as a sign proudly announced, was a brown brick building with glass windows that wrapped around a cylindrical corner, which rose much higher into the night sky than the rest of the building. A blue Greyhound sign sat above the glass entrance doors as we made our way inside.

The station sat quiet and dimmed. Multiple square pods were arranged in rows throughout the middle of the station. Seats were attached to each, giving the option to sit on any of the four sides. Plants grew from the center of each pod, doing their best to contrast the dull gray the rest of the interior provided. An older man sat slumped in the closest cluster of seats on the left side, but other than the younger guy working the ticket counter, he appeared to be the only inhabitant of the station.

Signs hung down from the ceiling near the edge of the station, each reading a gate number before giving way to a short hallway I guessed led to the buses themselves. In the far back of the station, construction tape surrounded building materials, some stacked on the floor, while others leaned against a tempo-rary wall that blocked off the corner of the station.

A deep baritone growl sounded from outside the station. It sounded metallic, like the one from earlier, but this one clearly came from something bigger. I looked around, but the station was creature-free, the growl seemingly echoing from everywhere. The station made me feel claustrophobic, like a trapped wild animal, but I didn't see any electricity-shooting cobras yet, so I was considering it a win.

We browsed the boards above the ticket counter, looking for the next bus that would keep us heading toward Denver. There weren't any great choices, as the next one didn't leave until 8:05 a.m., heading to Cleveland. Lucinda declared it our best option and started off toward the counter.

Before she could get there, a new sound arose from outside the station. I started to face it when the glass front doors exploded behind me, sending shards flying into the station. I ducked and covered my head, turning away from the blast. Pieces of glass peppered the bag and my shoulders, but none cut through my hoodie, feeling instead like someone was flicking me repeatedly.

More growling—I swear they had metal voice boxes—sounded from the now wide-open doors, and I turned to see two bright orange serpents, just as large as the one earlier, entering the station, slithering over the broken glass like it wasn't there. One already had a matching orange ball growing in its mouth, its eyes locked on me.

"*Dispergo!*" Lucinda yelled, which I took to mean something along the lines of "Get out of the way!"

She and Vincent grabbed Ollie and ran toward the ticket counter and the wide-eyed worker, while I turned to the square section of seats in front of me. My Glacies power flared up, telling me the orange ball was about to be launched. I steadied a foot on a seat and vaulted up and onto the middle of the seating arrangement. The ferns there grabbed at my clothes as I rolled off, landing on the seats on the other side before falling to the floor.

"Dammit!" I yelled. My side was never going to recover at this rate.

Maya flew over the seating arrangement and landed—much more smoothly than I did—next to me as flames licked over the plants with a whoosh.

Great, *these* shot fire.

I heard another fireball launch, again hearing the whoosh as it impacted somewhere else in the station. I peeked around the row of chairs, spotting both reptiles. One sat idle, waiting for Maya and me to appear from behind the seating area. The other one, which had just catapulted its fireball, was turning and joining its companion in its hunt for me.

A plan formed quickly.

I returned to cover and laid out my idea. Maya agreed to it, though I could tell she wasn't thrilled with the danger I was going to put us both in. I shed my bag as she brought her necklace out, her spear growing in her hand. The ring made me another sickle, though I opted for only one, as I'd need the free hand. I created an ice ball about the size of a baseball in that free hand and waited for Maya to put the plan in motion.

She took a deep breath, then leapt around the corner in the opposite direction of me. "Hey, hissy, over here!"

Seeing she'd caught the attention of the nearest snake, I threw my ice ball toward the other side of the station, where it shattered on hitting the wall. The far beast, alerted to the new sound, slithered in my direction, just like I'd hoped.

A fireball got launched at Maya, who rolled out of the way, and toward the older man, who was now wide awake, frozen in shock by the abnormally large serpents. I crouched low enough so my head didn't stick above the chairs and waited for snake number two to get closer.

I jumped out at the beast as it evened with me. It had a fireball ready in its mouth, but the surprise and proximity caused it to launch it just over my head and into the ceiling. I swung the sickle; its blade sliced through it with ease. A shriek—another sound I didn't know they could make—was cut short, and like the one in the courtyard, the creature shrank until only skin remained.

I returned my attention to Maya, who was drawing the action away from the terrified old man but was running out of room in the station to avoid the danger herself. Vincent leapt from the ticket counter and took off to help her. I sprinted toward the front of the station as well, forming another snowball and throwing it.

I'm not convinced I would've made a little league baseball team, much less a high school team. The ball of ice flew well wide of the snake, landing with a splat about ten feet away. It did turn its focus toward me, though. A growl rose from its throat as it formed a fireball.

A flash of light to my left drew me away, where a fireball was already being loaded by a third cobra, outside of the station. My heart stopped seeing it, already anticipating the heat.

The ticket counter was to my immediate left. Lucinda, with far more agility than I would've guessed possible, jumped over it and put herself between me and the danger, yelling in flurried Latin at me. Another blur of movement came from the right, and Vincent wrapped Lucinda in a bear hug, using his momentum to carry them both over and behind the counter, leaving me alone again.

The two cobras launched their fireballs at me simultaneously. They whistled in the air, each on a direct path to my heart. Regular human Jaden would've been dead.

But Maledictus was not. Glacies took over my body, clearing my mind, making it sharp. I threw myself to the ground as the two balls collided above me in a fiery explosion that singed my clothes and showered embers over me.

I was up and running as soon as the flames cleared. I needed to put distance between myself and the cobras, as well as draw them away from the others. I sprinted toward the back wall, ready to face them head-on.

Maya appeared at my side, slightly slower than me, but keeping up.

"I thought you were dead." She laughed, breathing hard.

Why are you laughing right now?

I had no idea how this crazy girl was laughing while being hunted by giant reptiles, but I smiled as I ran alongside. We heard a fireball launch from behind us. I jumped to the side, Maya doing the same thing. The ball raced between us, exploding against the concrete back wall.

Unfortunately, we were soon against that concrete wall. The serpents closed in, trapping us. This was the first time I'd gotten a real look at one without dodging a fireball. Their streamline bodies were a solid neon orange until they reached the head, where they were as black as the blade on Vincent's ax. I didn't think it was possible, but their eyes were an even darker black, like two pits staring into you, inviting you to jump.

Maya sidestepped her way past me, moving toward the construction area. The pair didn't pay her any attention; I realized they had cornered the prey they'd been after the whole time.

They hissed in unison, forming a word as they closed in. *Frosssssssssssttttttttt.*

Chills ran down my back as they hissed my name, which in turn made me mad. I can't explain exactly why. Maybe it was because I should've died three times already, once to Noah and twice to these stupid snakes. I'd survived so far, and while the score was technically two to zero in my favor, I knew my luck would run out.

Maya grabbed my attention with a "Pssst" to my left. I turned my head to see she had the door to the construction area open, heading through it to safety. I looked back, with hatred, toward the orange twins, who still sang my name. To my surprise, they backed up a couple of feet and stopped hissing, but soon started creating fireballs, readying to attack again. I dropped the sickle; it disappeared back into the ring before it even hit the ground. With both hands, I started forming an ice ball of my own, but it was purely for distraction.

When the ice was the size of a kickball, I lobbed it toward the snakes and sprinted for the door. Two fireballs shot at me as I dove through it. They exploded in the doorway, directly above me, the flames licking my neck and burning the hair off, singeing my skin. I heard a sound, like bricks falling on top of each other, and I curled into the fetal position as dust and debris crashed to the floor around me.

Soon, it stopped, the dust hanging in the air. I sat up, coughing and throwing pieces of rubble off me, to see that the temporary wall had crumbled, other building materials falling on top of it. The debris nearly reached the ceiling, allowing only a slimmer of light into the dark construction area.

I searched the rubble wall, looking for a way through, with no luck. We weren't getting back into the station that way. I hoped Lucinda and Vincent could protect Ollie until I could find a way back.

I turned to look deeper into the construction area, but the darkness only let me see ten feet in front of me. Maya was nowhere to be found, and a brief moment of panic welled in my throat that she had gotten trapped in the destruction. The sound of scuffling footsteps in the dark snuffed the fears.

The dust stung my burnt neck as I wandered in the dark. Freezing my hand, I used it as an icepack, the cold soothing the burning for now.

My search found a solid wall; scaffolding rose into the darkness, along with some other power tools and building materials scattered along it. I could hear noises around me, but the echoing of the empty area made it hard to pinpoint exactly where it was coming from.

"Frosty," Maya called out from around me. I squinted, looking for her, but couldn't find her.

"Where are you?" I asked.

"I'm over you."

"Like, emotionally?"

I audibly heard her face palm. "No, *gelida stultus,* look up."

"If you're going to insult me, can you at least do it in a language I understand?" I asked, looking up into the darkness. She appeared directly above me, hanging down from the top of the scaffolding.

"No, but thanks for asking. Maybe you could just learn it like everyone else does."

I scoffed, my reply ready, but she cut me off.

"Get up here. We're going to have to go this way."

I rolled my eyes as I climbed, still mad, but smirking just a little. I still didn't trust her, but as far as people go, she seemed pretty cool.

She helped pull me up the last level of the scaffolding, the rattling of the metal clanking off the cavernous ceiling that was lost way up in the darkness. The floor smelled of fresh wood and metal, making it obvious this level was under renovation as well. Beams of moonlight filtered in through glass windows, but they failed to offer more than spots of faint glow.

Maya smiled at me, but it melted quickly. She looked down at my chest, avoiding eye contact. "Are you mad?" she asked, seemingly randomly.

I frowned. Could she see that in the dark? "Yes."

"Why?" she asked, still looking at the center of my chest.

"Because everything has been trying to kill me since you guys got here. Those… things knew who I was; they actually hissed my name. Noah shows up right before you do, posing as my babysitter's son, saying he knows who I am, right before he tried to kill me. Everyone seems to know who I am but me."

"I understand this is a lot, but you need to relax," she said, putting her hand on my shoulder, which was not a way to make me relax. "Your eyes are completely white."

I didn't understand what that had to do with anything, so I said nothing.

She sighed, removing her hand and turning around. "We know little about your curse, but one thing we know is that when you get mad, your eyes will turn white, and it'll freeze anything that makes eye contact with you for too long."

This sounded awesome to me, but she still seemed worried about it.

"I've seen what happens to a person who looks too long," she continued. "Ian will sometimes freeze those he can't get to join him."

My gut feeling was the person she was referring to wasn't just anyone, but I didn't press.

"Will you lead? I can barely see," she said now.

I adjusted my eyes to the darkness, which amazingly let me see more than I could before, so I stepped in front of her.

We walked forward carefully, scanning the ground in front to avoid stepping on any loose nails or other dangerous objects. We made it not even fifty feet into the large, open second floor when the metallic growl I'd grown to loathe pulsed off the walls.

The deeper, thicker growl I'd heard earlier rattled the floor under us, turning my anger into fear. Metal pipes, paint cans, and other objects crashed to the ground in the distance. There was something big, and it was up here with us, slithering around in the dark.

We crept forward, my eyes flickering back and forth, looking for any movement. The low roar still sent shivers down my spine as I snuck through the darkness. Any other noise up here was completely drowned out.

A crash up and to my left made me steer us toward the right, where a bunch of building materials lay stacked in neat piles, ready to be placed on the walls and floor. We made no noise as we weaved between the piles.

The growling stopped, and the only sound in the silence became my shaky breath. I was completely terrified. Still, I tiptoed forward, Maya right behind me, an unspoken agreement that we both wanted to get back downstairs as soon as possible.

We were nearing the edge of the stacked materials. Beyond, the floor reopened up into what I guessed was going to be another waiting area, but with no furniture, I couldn't tell. I stared into the dark, looking for anything, even an outline, resembling a massive reptile.

I passed one of the final pallet stacks when sawdust exploded into the air beside me. Pallets tumbled as a cobra launched its body over the stack, its mouth open, fangs glistening in the moonlight. I fell backward, twisting my body to face it while bringing my hands in front of me.

Back on the first floor, my Glacies power saved me from certain death. This time, however, I can say proudly I was responsible for my own quick thinking. I threw my hands up at the attacking snake, forming a jagged icicle from the palm of my hand. It pierced through the roof of its mouth, passing through the rest of its head, killing it instantly. Its body had already turned to dead skin by the time it landed on me, which I quickly brushed off as I stood.

"Are you o—" Maya started, before a deafening roar cut her off.

We both turned as the source slithered into view.

A titanic black cobra, at least fifteen feet tall and thicker around than I was, finished its roar, its hood flapping, creating a sound like helicopter blades. It spotted us with its giant eyes and let out another roar; the obnoxiously loud sound a mix of T-Rex and Godzilla, at least from all the movies I'd ever seen. A swirling black cloud formed in its mouth as it roared. A green light appeared, growing in vibrance as the cloud grew in size. I'd seen enough to know what was about to happen.

"*Id est magnus asinus anguis,*" Maya muttered behind me.

I ducked behind a pile of thick stone flooring slabs as the roar finished. A brilliant green flash illuminated the walls around me as the stone slabs disintegrated into black ash, leaving me exposed, the monster already forming another cloud.

I raced across the floor, darting behind a concrete mixer as the cloud fired again. It, too, ended up a pile of black ash, forcing me to continue my mad dash away from the death laser.

I hadn't seen Maya since I'd avoided the first shot, but I hoped she was trying to sneak around the beast, because I was going to run out of things to hide behind.

A stack of plywood instantly got vaporized, so I moved to the next one, but kept going, moving to the darkened side of the room, the windows here covered with tarps. Ten feet behind me, the second stack of plywood vaporized. I moved forward, keeping my body low as I weaved between more materials, lying flat behind a row of toolboxes, waiting for the next laser.

I waited for ten seconds, then another ten. Still no laser. I risked peeking my head up. The brute swept side to side, its tongue flicking in and out, as it slithered into the middle of the clearing to my right, trying to find me in the congestion.

The ring formed the sickle in my hand again as I lay there. Every part of me wanted to sneak past the monster instead of fighting it, but I knew it would find me again on the first floor, and I had no clue where Maya had gone. I didn't want to leave her alone; I hoped she felt the same way.

My sixth sense, now the Glacies power, ran through scenarios in my head. Eventually, it settled on the best option, though it didn't seem thrilled about my odds, either. I timed my movement with the snake, moving closer as it looked away, then ducking down as it would look back and search in the darkness.

I hid behind a support pillar, the last cover between me and the angrily growling serpent only fifteen feet away. I wasn't sure how much damage I could do in one swing to the giant, so I decided I would employ the "death by a thousand cuts" strategy, hiding and attacking from the shadows as many times as necessary.

I got ready for my first attempt, grabbing a nearby brick. I took off my hoodie, rubbing my face on it to get as much of my scent as possible, recalling something about snakes having a good sense of smell. Next, I wrapped it tightly around the brick and stood once it looked away from me again.

I chucked the brick as far as I could. It sailed silently through the night until it crashed against the other wall with a muffled thud before falling onto a stack of paint cans, creating a lot more noise.

I was up and running as the beast roared and fired a laser in the direction of the noise. A sickle appeared in my other hand, and I raised both, ready to slash as I passed its back.

And then I was blinded. Light poured in from beyond the snake, powerful enough to light the entire room. Dark shadows were cast up the walls from the pillars and materials as they gleamed in the light. Not that I could see anything. The intense blue color of my eyes helped me see in the dark, but I'd learned multiple times it made them extremely sensitive to light.

My vision was completely white, any ability to see in the dark completely flooded out. I stumbled backward and into the pillar, tracing my hand around it as I felt my way to where I hoped to put it between me and the cobra, who roared at the sudden brightness. I rubbed my eyes hard, willing the spots to go away. It helped, but a large whited-out blotch still blocked the center of my vision.

I was trying to blink the spot away when I heard a sickening stabbing sound, followed by a pained roar. My brain put the pieces together: Maya must've turned the light on and was now fighting the beast. I needed to help her.

It was a good thing Maya had been a distraction, as I discovered I wasn't fully behind the pillar, leaving half my body exposed to the laser. I stepped out fully now, turning my head at an angle to see the reptile out of the side of my eye.

Half-running, half-stumbling, I moved toward it; trying to run in one direction while only able to look out of the corner of your eye isn't easy. I slashed at its back with both sickles, the tips digging into the skin and slicing through flesh as I raced past.

The titan roared, firing a laser wildly that landed a foot in front of me, creating a small hole in the floor. I kept moving to a pillar near the outside edge of the light, which I could now see came from a tripod stand with multiple construction lights hanging from it. I scooted down to my butt, trying to make myself small in case a laser went through the pillar.

Maya didn't give it a chance. I watched her as she dipped in and out of my blind spot, hopping over fallen debris as she ran up silently from behind, jumping to grab her spear, which was lodged in the scaly midsection, twisting as she removed it. The snake howled in pain again, thoroughly pissed off.

A very stupid idea popped into my head. I holstered the sickles, sending them back into the ring, instead opting for a different tool. Unfortunately, I didn't know the exact name of it, but I pictured it in my mind, hoping the ring would somehow be able to give me what I wanted.

At first, nothing happened. Then they appeared in my hands. I admired them briefly, running my finger along the serrated blade until it met the tip and curved back around. They were uncommon in DC due to the lack of attractions in the area, but these ice axes were going to climb a different material today.

I stood back up, chuckling at the absurdity of what I was about to attempt. Best case, I lived up to being *Maledictus.* Worst case, well, almost certain death. But I was beginning to trust my powers, and in turn, myself.

Maya still held the irritated cobra's attention, so I made my move. The blind spot was shrinking in size, but still very much annoying in the middle of my vision.

I leapt as I reached the serpent, digging both axes in as far as they would go. It hissed, and I hung on tightly, spinning with it as it turned to where the pain was, unaware that I was attached. When it stopped, I used my feet on its scales, getting a surprisingly good grip, propelling upward, removing the axes as I jumped. I planted them again, this time near the base of its neck.

By now, the monster was aware of the pest clinging to it. It shook, trying to throw me off, but I used the momentum to swing under it, bringing the right axe across its neck and attaching to the other side. My left hand let go of its axe, leaving it impaled.

I dangled fifteen feet above the ground, holding on for dear life as the snake tried to buck me off. My grip was loosening, sliding down as the sweat and movement lowered my hand. An idea occurred, one that I realized I'd been unknowingly practicing not too long ago. I froze my hand to the axe, and instantly the sliding stopped. I used the rejuvenated grip to pull my body up, swinging my legs to straddle the cobra just above the hood, which fluttered violently, creating a surprising amount of wind. Squeezing tight with my legs, I reached down to my ankle, removing Noah's dagger from where it sat in its sheath.

The scales on the dagger flapped open as it arced into the creature's skull.

Ironic, I thought as I pushed the blade with all my strength, driving down to the hilt. Underneath me, the beast tensed before going limp.

My stupid plan had worked. Unfortunately, because it was a stupid plan, this was as far as it went. Never in my life did I have a problem with gravity, but as the ground quickly approached while I clung to the neck of the lifeless giant beneath me, it became issue number one.

As I plummeted down, I prepared to jump off at the last

moment, seeing no alternative to a crash landing. Steeling myself, I leapfrogged off the cobra right before it hit the ground, pushing off the animal to avoid getting crushed by it. I braced for impact, slamming my knee on the ground, falling into a barrel roll that lasted several feet until a pile of two-by-fours stopped my momentum.

I lay on my back, catching my breath for a moment. A shadow rose over the ceiling, and Maya appeared above me, an incredulous look on her face. She extended a hand, helping me up to my feet. Her face was a foot from mine, staring at me with a mix of disbelief and ridicule. She brushed the hair that stuck to my forehead, still saying nothing. I stood still, more afraid to move now than I'd been against the massive cobra. Apparently, the Glacies power isn't all that helpful for social interactions.

"Close your mouth. You look like a moron," she said.

I hadn't even realized it was open. Slowly, I closed it, mumbling, "Sorry."

She laughed, moving her hand to my shoulder. I tensed up, so she took her hand off. "That was one of the dumbest things I've seen someone do in a long time."

"I mean, I thought it was kinda cool," I said, shaken from my trance. I looked at the dead skin on the ground. "Plus, it worked."

"Can't argue with that. We should probably get back to the others before anything else shows up."

It was quiet the rest of the way through the second floor. There was another set of stairs at the far edge of the station, open, and as far as I could tell, not under construction. They led us back down, where the first floor was almost unrecognizable. All the lights were on, and the station was filled with people.

Cops, reporters, and curious citizens milled about, looking for information on what happened.

Maya pulled me aside by the arm, dragging me into a storage closet. As she did, I caught a glimpse of Ollie. He stood next to Lucinda and Vincent, who now wore my bag on his back. They stood in front of a cop, who pointed at a snakeskin, asking them questions. Maya locked the door and turned the light off behind us. My vision had gone back to normal, and I could just make out features on her face from the slim beam of light that leaked underneath the door, so I was fairly confident she couldn't see much, if anything.

"You need to change," Maya said. "I can smell your clothes from here."

It's difficult to change when you have nothing to change into. But before I could tell her that, she told me to wait, and walked confidently into the station, closing the door behind her. I sat in the darkness, freezing and unfreezing my hand to pass the time.

She returned ten minutes later with the backpack.

"Sorry, I talked with the people you guys call 'cops,' and they asked a lot of questions," she said as she shut the door behind her, returning the closet to darkness. "Asked me if I'd seen a boy about my age with blond hair and a scar near his temple. Don't worry, I told them I hadn't, but you should probably hang in here for a while."

I thanked her for grabbing my bag, and for not turning me in, and then headed toward the back of the storage closet. It was dark enough back there that even I couldn't see anything.

Digging into my bag, I found a new pair of pants and changed. I took off my t-shirt, but before I put the clean one on, I felt down along my sides, feeling all the new scrapes and

84

bumps. They stung as I grazed them, reminding me of what I'd gone through in the past twenty-four hours.

For the first time, though, I thought of the future, and meeting my mother. A strange feeling gripped my heart, and I shook my head. *Careful,* I warned myself. She probably had three heads and a pair of wings. It would be a miracle if she didn't try to eat me.

I looked blindly in my bag for a hoodie, my hand rummaging through wads of clothes, until it hit a soft cotton fabric. I squeezed it, knowing what it was.

It was a light-baby-blue hoodie that Mr. Alvarez sneaked into my bag the day I left his house. I had arrived at my next stop in the foster-care system that I'd grown to hate by the time I found it. There was a saying that was used around the Alvarez house, mainly by Mr. Alvarez whenever something went wrong. With twelve kids, he used it a lot. *Learn to dance, Jaden,* he would say, something about not waiting for storms to pass, but instead going outside and dancing in the rain.

I would always roll my eyes, but the saying stuck.

The front had a small white cloud in the chest area, raindrops falling from it. The drops fell onto the words "Learn to Dance," the bottom of the letters melting away, as if the rain was dripping off them.

It had been way too big to begin with, but it was getting tighter on me as I grew. As far as adult figures in my life went, he was one of the better ones, and I wasn't willing to let the hoodie go anytime soon. My fingers traced the scar on my forearm, my mind flashing back to that night. I pushed the thoughts aside, threw on the hoodie, and returned to the front of the closet.

Maya sat leaning against a wall. I took a seat against the wall opposite her.

"Back when we got attacked by the first snake, you guessed it wouldn't be normal, and you were right. How'd you know?" I asked her.

"Remember how I told you that Desolates can get inside of people's minds and, in a way, control them after some time? Powerful Desolates can do that with animals, too, except animals are much easier to gain control over."

"Okay, but that doesn't explain how they could shoot fire or electricity or be big enough to swallow me in one bite."

"Very powerful Desolates can manipulate them, make them more dangerous."

"So those cobras were created by a Desolate?"

"I'm guessing they were once normal, but a Desolate changed them to become what we fought against."

"All just to try to stop me, us, from getting back?"

She nodded.

For a while, we said nothing. The buzz from the station made me nod off, but I twitched myself awake, rubbing my eyes in the dark.

"Did you sleep on the train?" Maya asked, her voice soft in the quiet closet.

"No."

"Then go to sleep," she said. "Vincent said he would get us when the crowd dies down or our bus is about to leave."

I reluctantly agreed, pulled my hood over my head, and found as comfortable a position as I could with my back against a concrete wall. After a few moments of silence, I asked, "How old are you, anyway?"

"Sixteen," she said.

"Is time the same in Arrortha?"

"Yes."

"So I won't be, like, one hundred years old when I get there?"

I heard her laugh from across the room. "Not quite."

"That's good to know," I said, closing my eyes.

Unlike on the train, sleep soon claimed me.

Chapter Seven

Maya gently shook me awake a few hours later. Light entered the supply closet through the now open door, though a big, tall silhouette standing in the doorway blocked some of it. The figure entered the closet, and as the face leaned closer, I could tell it was Vincent.

"Did you two have fun in here?" he asked, looking over cleaning supplies on the shelf beside me.

Maya rolled her eyes as she helped me to my feet, punching him in the arm before turning to exit the closet.

Vincent smirked at me as I turned to follow her.

The station was buzzing with the overnight events, adding to the passengers arriving for their morning commutes. News channels did live reports, recapping the events and looking for anyone who was present, asking them for live interviews.

I could see three reporters by the ticket counter, each holding some sort of recording device, interviewing the young overnight worker. He spoke with exaggerated hand movements, though I was too far away to hear his words.

I kept my hood up, remembering Maya's description of the kid the police wanted to question, which matched me pretty well. I stared at my feet as we walked behind a reporter doing a live interview with a police officer.

"The group entered the station around two-forty-five a.m.," the cop said. "They broke the glass doors before unleashing wild animals inside of the station."

"Can you tell us about the destruction caused to the station?" the reporter asked, egging the cop to tell everything he knew.

"They lit a construction wall on fire, which has now collapsed. However, there is no danger to the integrity of the rest of the building. This is an ongoing investigation. I'm sorry, that is all I can tell you."

"What about suspects?" the reporter asked as the cop began to walk away.

Yeah, me, I thought as we passed directly behind them.

"We are reviewing security footage, but at this time, witnesses say the main suspect is a teenage boy with blond hair and a noticeable scar on his face. We are working to confirm this," he said, speed walking away before the reporter asked any more questions.

We weaved through reporters, cops, and travelers, finding Lucinda and Ollie tucked into seats in front of one of the farthest gates.

Ollie perked up when he saw me alive, but Lucinda shushed him to avoid drawing attention. I sat down next to her as Vincent took the seat next to me, hovering way too close, but doing his best to shield me from any cameras that may have been panning the station.

Lucinda had bought tickets for the 8:05 bus for Cleveland. I risked peeking at a clock on the wall, where its illuminated face showed it was barely past 7:00 a.m.

The next hour went painfully slowly. I rested my forehead on my bag, which sat in my lap, hoping this would shield me from every direction. Vincent occasionally whispered, "Stay down," which I assume was anytime a camera got too close for comfort, though I'd no intentions of showing my face.

At one point, I asked Vincent to get Maya's attention, and shortly after, I could feel her presence as she leaned in close enough to where we could talk quietly. I asked her about removing the scar, since that would be the easiest thing anyone looking for the cop's suspect could identify me with. She told me we had waited too long, and since she had healed me for something else, she couldn't go back and remove it. But she did offer to take me to one of the oldest healers in Highmoore, who *was* strong enough to remove it. Which wasn't too helpful for my current situation, but I didn't tell her that. She returned to her seat, and I returned to counting the passing seconds in my head.

Finally, the attendant called to board the bus to Cleveland. We were first, moving through the short hallway into a darkened parking garage as Lucinda passed off the tickets to the gate worker.

A cop watched on, eyeing the passengers as they entered the bus. I kept my eyes forward, never making eye contact with him, and it seemed to work, as he headed back into the station once the bulk of the passengers produced their tickets.

I eyed each passenger from the back of the bus as they got

on. There were only a handful, as the bus to Cleveland was not a popular route, especially with the chaos in the station. An older couple, tourists, were the first to sit a couple of seats in front of us. A couple of men, each talking on their cell phones, boarded, but they showed no interest in anyone and sat near the front. A few single riders hopped on, but none caught my attention.

The doors were about to close when a final passenger jumped on, thanking the bus driver with a smile for waiting. He had to be in his late fifties, wearing jeans and a simple sweater vest over a white shirt as he walked slowly up the aisle, scanning each rider as he shuffled by them. His face showed content, like he was just happy to be there, but scanning each rider told me he was looking for someone, and I had a bad feeling I knew who.

He stopped halfway down the aisle, his eyes moving to the back of the bus where we sat. He locked on me, his mouth opening into a toothy smile, a look of pleasant surprise on his face, as if he had run into a close friend at the grocery store.

Quite the chaos you're causing, Maledictus.

Like before, I heard the words clearly in my head, but he spoke to me without speaking. My blood ran cold as he continued.

Your curse has made you strong, but your inexperience has made you oblivious to the truth. You must be smart in who you choose to believe, Jaden. They won't hesitate to get rid of you once your usefulness is gone, just like they did with me. We're a danger to them. I trust you will choose my offer when the time comes.

With that, he sat down, his wispy brown hair peeking over the top of the seat.

"Esham," Vincent muttered beside me.

"Huh?"

"That man's name is Esham. He's Ian's top advisor. He must really want you if he's willing to send him."

"A real troublemaker, that one," Lucinda added.

I didn't know whether to feel honored or continue being scared.

"Did he say anything to you, in your mind?" Lucinda asked now.

I gawked at her, giving away the answer without saying anything. How could she have possibly known?

"He used to work for me, but left with Ian," she continued. "He'd use his little mind trick when he couldn't wait to speak with me in private. What did he say?"

The pair looked at me expectantly, Maya joining them.

"He said I was causing a lot of chaos," I said, starting slowly. Nobody interrupted me, so I kept going. "He basically said I didn't know what the truth was, and that he trusted me to accept his offer. What offer?"

"He's trying to recruit you," Vincent said matter-of-factly. "I would guess Ian sent him to get you to join him."

"How would that help him?" I asked.

Maya said, "Think of everything you can do. Wouldn't you want you on your side? He's spent the last fifteen years trying to convince everyone that you are the only thing he needs to take back Highmoore and therefore Arrortha. But at the same time, he's also convinced too many people that you and your mother are the only ones standing in his way. With the fact you're both cursed, I'm guessing he thinks he can convince you to side with him."

"Isn't he the one who cursed me?"

"He's influential. I never said he was smart," she said with a smile.

* * *

The next hour crawled by slower than the one in the station did. All of us were on guard, ready if Esham were to try anything. He never so much as moved, though, and soon we were in the outer districts of Cleveland, downtown looming out of the driver's windshield.

As we approached, I leaned over to Vincent, asking a question that had been on my mind. "I know we have Ollie, but if there are four of us and one of him, why are we so afraid of him?"

"Hey!" Ollie said. "I can help, too."

"I like where your head's at," Vincent said, his face unreadable. "I don't mean to be harsh, but I won't sugarcoat it for you. You don't understand the powers, or what he's capable of. And that's not your fault, but it's something you need to learn. Look at everyone on this bus."

I scanned the other passengers, but still none seemed to pose much of a threat or take an interest in the other riders.

"You don't know how many are working with him. Beyond that, he spoke inside your mind, right?"

"Yeah."

"That's difficult for a normal Desolate to do to a non-Desolate, but you're next to impossible to have this effect on. That alone should scare you. It scares me, and he hasn't even tried it on me. Plus, he can control the other passengers easily. Remember how Noah controlled your babysitter? It's the same thing. Even if he were alone, you'd have to fight through every helpless human on this bus. I've got no doubt you could do it without breaking a sweat, but if you're willing to, maybe you're more like Ian than I originally thought."

There was no way I was willing to, and I told him so. He agreed I seemed better than that, though I could tell he didn't trust any of the powers, let alone a kid with all of them. Maybe we weren't so different after all.

After some silence, I asked him, "Why didn't you want a power?"

"Because they're not natural. Don't get me wrong, the ability to make ice or move stone with my mind would be cool. But the odds of getting one of those are already low, and making plants or healing people isn't interesting to me. And I already paid someone to make me a metal weapon, so I don't need the Ferrum power. Unlike everyone else, I can say that everything I do is done by me, that I'm more powerful than even those with a power. What about you? Would you have taken one, had you been given a choice?"

Would I?

I nodded.

"Most do."

* * *

Half an hour later, we pulled into the Cleveland bus station. The driver had just opened the doors when Esham exited the bus without a glance back. I watched him through my window as he disappeared into the station.

We were the last passengers on the bus. The driver looked at us with annoyance before he, too, gave a slight shrug and left the bus, entering the station to grab a coffee before his next trip.

Lucinda guided us through the bus parking lot. After a couple of weird looks from the workers, we exited into the street in front of the station.

We agreed we needed to get out of the city and find another way to keep moving toward Denver, as Esham would be gathering people to stop us. We decided on Chicago as our next stop. I told Lucinda it wasn't on the way to Denver, but she thought this was a good thing, as it would hopefully throw Esham off.

We walked the streets for at least an hour, looking for any method of transportation. We hailed a taxi, but the driver yelled at us for wasting his time and sped off when we asked him to take us to a different city.

Finally, we found a building with a sign that read "Travel Ohio!" As we entered the building, an overly perky woman welcomed us in, her earrings bouncing with each word she said to us.

"We need to get out of the city," I said to her, sitting in the chair she had motioned me to. Lucinda sat next to me while Ollie took the other side. Vincent and Maya looked out the window.

"Well, you came to the right place, sweetheart! I'm Kendra; I own this place," the woman bubbled. "How far are you looking to go?"

"Just out of the city for now," I said.

"I can do that for you! You're not in any trouble, are you darling?" she asked, eyeing Lucinda.

Lucinda glared back, clearly not enjoying the questions.

"Not at all! We just need to get to—" I panicked, looking at the giant map of the state that hung beside us. "Columbus, for my, uh, sister's birthday. It's a surprise party."

I hoped my face wasn't too red, but if it was, Kendra gave no indication.

"A surprise party? I love those! I'm an expert planner! Anyway, I can get you five tickets to Columbus, no problem. There's a bus leaving from a stop a few blocks down in an hour. I can put you on it!"

"We'll take it," Lucinda said.

"Great! That'll be two hundred seventy-six dollars. Cash or card?"

I coughed when I heard the price, but Lucinda calmly pulled out a wad of bills from the bag and handed them to me to count for her. Kendra raised her eyebrows at the mass of cash, curious at the size of it. I handed her three one-hundred-dollar bills. After holding them up the light and giving them a thorough inspection, they seemed real enough to her.

"Amazing," she said, after giving us the tickets. "The bus stop is four blocks to the south. You can't miss it! You and those pearly blues come back anytime!"

Even after buying the tickets, I thought the stack of cash was plenty to get us to Denver. I gave the bills back to Lucinda as we thanked Kendra and headed out the door to the south, hoping to find an empty bus stop.

We had no such luck. At least twenty-five people waited for the bus, spilling out onto the sidewalk once the covered bench was full. There were a few clouds in the sky, but the sun shone through, so we didn't mind waiting outside. We pressed ourselves up against a building to let pedestrians pass through, as well as keep an eye on all the passengers waiting.

Vincent and Lucinda spoke to each other, so I joined in with Maya and Ollie, who were mid-conversation. Maya was describing the other kids in Arrortha, and how they were like Ollie, who would make a ton of good friends. Ollie was eating all of it up, asking about where he would live, and if he and I would still be brothers. Maya answered with an emphatic yes and went on to describe the grand castle he would live in. She was an excellent storyteller, and I soon listened intently, asking questions whenever I could think of any.

Not long into her describing the city, a figure walking toward us stole my attention. The boy seemed to be my age, maybe a little younger, and he stared at the ground as he walked, where I saw he was barefoot. His arms were crossed over his chest, covering a torn black shirt. A mess of brown hair swayed as he walked, moving side to side with his head. Although I couldn't hear him over the rest of the crowd, it looked like he was talking to himself as he approached.

He closed to within twenty feet without looking up. I'd tuned out the other conversation, focusing fully on the kid. He looked up, making my stomach drop. He had dark, sullen and sad eyes that appeared darker against his pasty skin. What terrified me the most was the rest of his face. He looked eerily like an older, but deathly sick version of Ollie. He approached, eyes locked on mine, before turning and running straight at my brother. As he closed, his arms unfolded, revealing a short knife that glinted in the sun. A yellow liquid dripped off the tip of the blade, falling to the concrete below.

I pushed Ollie aside as the boy swung the weapon. My shove made Ollie avoid serious harm, but the blade still sliced through his right bicep, and he cried out in pain. Maya threw herself between my brother and the kid, shoving him backward and onto the ground. He hopped right back up and took off before she could grab him. I raced after him with no idea what I was going to do if I caught him.

We weaved through the street, avoiding honking cars and screaming cyclists. I pushed my legs as fast as they would go, but the barefoot kid pulled away from me, freakishly fast as he danced around and in between cars.

He turned down a side street, and I couldn't see him until I rounded the corner. He was halfway to the next intersection already, but between him and me were three men, all identical.

Now, when I say identical, I mean *identical.* They wore the same clothes, had the same face, and even moved the same. They strode toward me, all swinging their swords in the same direction at the same time. I jumped back, ready to draw my own weapon, but they swung again, impossibly fast. I dropped to my hands and knees under this attack, having to stay down longer to avoid all three swords. The first sword slammed into the ground, feet from where I was. The second slammed down a moment later, inches away. I knew the third one would hit me if I didn't move, so I rolled away as it smashed down right where I'd been.

Somebody's arms wrapped around me as I climbed back to my feet. The three guys were too close, and I couldn't break free as they all swung in unison. I watched the middle sword arc toward my neck, and I tried to bring my hands up to create an ice shield, but whoever was behind me held them tight. I flinched, ready for the pain I knew was coming.

The sword reached me, and to my astonishment, passed right through me. I felt no pain, only confusion, as the sword retracted and all three men stepped back, standing impossibly still.

"Let go of me!" I screamed, thrashing around in the arms of my captor.

"Calm down," Vincent said behind me.

"They're going to kill me!"

"Who? There is nobody here."

I looked at the men, clear as day, in front of me. But as I began to tell the blind guy behind me about them, the three men evaporated, blown away like leaves in the wind.

"They… there were…. What?" I stammered.

Join us and learn the truth.

Esham's voice echoed in my head, and I spotted him near the intersection a block away from us. The boy stood next to him, still holding the knife.

Join us, Maledictus.

With that, he turned and disappeared behind a building, along with the kid.

I finally broke free from Vincent's firm grasp, turning to face him. Lucinda stood next to him, a concerned look on her face.

"Your brother needs you. Now," she said, turning and heading back toward Ollie. I followed behind, worry overtaking the confusion in my mind.

An even larger crowd had gathered at the bus stop, now huddled around something on the sidewalk. I pushed my way through the mass of bodies, finally reaching the front. My stomach dropped when I saw what everyone was looking at.

Maya knelt next to Ollie, who was on all fours himself. He was ghostly pale, sweat dripping off his face and onto the sidewalk. Blood ran from his bicep, streaking down his arm. Drool slipped from his mouth, running off his lips and pooling at the base of his chin. He looked as sick as the boy who attacked him.

I knelt next to him as the crowd continued to look on. Someone shouted, asking if anyone was a doctor. Others shouted to call 9-1-1. Beside me, Ollie wheezed through it all, struggling to breathe.

"The knife," Maya said, grabbing my arm to make sure I heard her. "The knife was poisoned."

I nodded to her, then put my hand on Ollie's arm, on top of the gash. He winced in pain, then coughed as he lost control of his breath again. I closed my eyes, focusing, like how I did on the train, though I was hoping for significantly better results. Maya saw what I was doing, because she leaned close and spoke softly in my ear.

"Think about healing him; take the poison. Small amounts, Jaden. Don't do too much."

I dragged him into this. I'm the cursed one, not him. No, I'm taking all of it.

Immediately, I felt a burning sensation in my right bicep, right where his cut was. The poison flowed through my shoulder and into my chest, stinging as it went. Sweat began to form on my forehead. Still, I continued. I tried to get all of it, my body growing weaker the more I took.

The whole thing took less than five seconds. Somewhere in the middle, Maya yelled at me to stop, but I ignored her.

I leaned back now as the world spun. Disfigured voices and gasps erupted from the crowd as Ollie sat up, looking normal. Though his arm seemed to shake, I couldn't even see a scar.

Maya asked me questions, but her voice sounded muffled, and I couldn't form a reply if I wanted to. I just stared into space, the world around me incoherent.

Despite the haziness, I could see genuine worry on her face as she put her hand on my chest. The sensation I'd felt when she healed me before cooled my chest, and the world focused a little.

"Can you hear me?" she asked.

I nodded.

"Did you take all of it?"

I nodded.

She muttered something in Latin, either about how amazing I was or how stupid I was. My guess is the second one.

I heard lots of shouting behind me, and I turned my head to see Vincent and Lucinda trying to keep the astonished crowd back, baffled by how the sick kid was now perfectly fine. It was clear they were going to lose, and they turned to us, yelling that we needed to go.

So much for the bus.

Maya tried to help me to my feet, but the poison was regaining control, and she had to drag me as I stumbled along with her. Ollie pushed his head up and under my other arm, willing me to keep moving.

"Come on!" he'd say whenever I stumbled.

We limped on a few blocks. Some of the crowd followed for a while, but as time neared for the bus to arrive, they too returned to the stop.

A few blocks later, we found a covered parking garage and ducked inside. Each step seemed to make me dizzier, and soon my world spun unbelievably fast, forcing me to close my eyes to avoid throwing up. Maya and Ollie strained to carry me, and they had to set me down, leaning me against a concrete pillar. I tried to say I was fine, but the words were embarrassingly slurred and foreign to me.

The poison was making my head pound. It stung my veins,

making every little movement difficult. Maya knelt in front of me, looking directly at me as she spoke, but the words were muffled and made no sense; she might as well have been speaking Latin to me. I stared blankly back at her. She rolled her eyes when she realized her patient hadn't understood a word she said and reached out toward my chest. I tried to tell her I was fine, and held up my arm to block her, but she swatted it away, annoyed. She took a little of the poison away, grimacing while she did so. Once she was done, the world came back into focus.

"I'm keeping you alive, you cursed idiot," she said as she ripped the bag off my shoulders and grabbed a t-shirt from it, wiping my face and neck. The shirt came back soaked.

Just then, the car next to us chirped and started as a sharply dressed businessman walked toward us, using the remote start on his keychain. He eyed us with suspicion, trying to figure out what our odd group was up to. Lucinda didn't waste a second walking up to meet him.

"How many Earth dollars for you to drive us to Chicago?" she asked.

I hung my head and sighed.

"To Chicago? That's not close, and I have two meetings this afternoon," he said, not even bothering to stop.

She walked alongside him, bringing out the wad of bills. "How many do you need? I have a lot."

He clicked his key chain again, and the car chirped throughout the garage. "I drive a BMW. I don't need your money. Go buy a bus ticket." He hopped in his car and sped off, leaving us alone in the garage again.

"I can drive you folks there. I'm heading to Indianapolis first, but it'll only be a quick pit stop," someone said.

I looked up to see a tall, skinny guy with a poorly cut mullet and matching facial hair.

Lucinda walked to meet him, and the two of them spoke briefly. He held up his hands, feigning surrender a couple of times, smiling while he did it. Her staff occasionally glowed as she questioned him, but soon enough, she handed him a wad of cash and motioned for us to follow her as he pointed to a rusted van parked close by.

The world continued to spin as I stood up. Maya kept putting her hand on my shoulder to steady me, and I shook her off each time.

"I can make it on my own," I said, though I stumbled, almost falling as I did. The poison clouded my mind, and I wasn't used to how much help she was already giving me.

"Stop acting like Vincent," she said sharply, frustrated with me. But eventually she gave up the fight.

I got close enough to the man that I could see the scraggly facial hair he wore through the waves of dizziness. He was tall and lanky, and he eyed me with curiosity, but shrugged his shoulders and hopped in the driver's seat as we climbed into the back of a rusted panel van.

The guy was obviously living in it. Clothes hung from a bar near the window, being utilized as curtains as well as a makeshift closet. A cot lay on the opposite side, the sheets folded neatly on top. Besides the stains on the floor and ceiling and the funky smell, the living area of the van was tidy and clean.

"My name's Hugo," he said, looking at us in the rearview mirror. "You can just call me Hu… or Go. Or just 'dude' if you want. I'm not picky. There are some seats behind me you folks can snag, although one of you might need to sit up front with me. Don't worry, I got my rabies shot just last week."

Small folding chairs were arranged behind the driver's and passenger's seats, for guests. Ollie climbed up front before any of us could stop him, getting a high five and a "'Sup, little dude?" from Hugo.

We pulled out of the parking garage as we sat down. I started to take off my bag before realizing it wasn't on my shoulders.

"Hey, H—" An intense and fiery pain flared in my chest before I could finish the name.

I shuffled into the living quarters of the van, grabbing at my chest. Maya left her seat to help me as the pain forced me flat on my back. She asked me questions, but I was unable to form a single word to answer. I gasped for air, the pain in my chest growing, like a massive anvil had been placed on top of me, each breath only increasing its weight.

Maya touched my chest, removing some of the poison. The pain eased slightly, but a wheezing sound escaped with every breath.

"Your amigo doesn't look too hot," Hugo said from up front.

"He got poisoned," I heard Ollie say. "Well, actually I did, but he has magic powers, so now I'm fine."

"That's neat, little dude!"

The van rolled through downtown Cleveland. I could just make out buildings through the dirty windows before Lucinda pulled the clothes close together, blocking the view.

Painful minutes passed as we exited the main part of the city. I threatened to lose consciousness, but each time I got close, Maya would take a little more poison or poke me until I got annoyed enough to stay awake. For what felt like an hour, this continued as we progressed toward our detour of Indianapolis.

Maya scolded me each time she had to take more poison, and even she was starting to sweat and look ill from the effects.

"I'm okay," I said.

"You're not okay, Jaden. You'd have been dead in the parking garage if I hadn't kept healing you. You have to learn to control your powers or this is going to happen."

I tried to tell her why I did it but was too weak to argue.

Eventually, her healing lost its effect, and she'd take some of the poison to no avail. The effects grew worse: My whole body ached, and chills swept through me and made me shiver. Maya dabbed sweat from my face, though soon the t-shirt she used was completely soaked. She looked around before saying, "I think we left your bag."

I nodded weakly.

I stared at the stains on the roof as each one danced, changing shape and color. A round one spun and switched from brown to a bright orange, rising high above an amoeba that transformed into a hieroglyphic man wielding a sword, who was attacked by another figure that appeared from a different stain. The two figures, both enshrouded in white, swung their swords at each other, new stains appearing where they met. They fought across the entire ceiling, neither gaining an edge.

My attention was drawn away from the fight by another silhouette, this one smaller than the two others, and black. It appeared to be holding something, and it cowered as the first two fought around it. Flashes of gray, white, and green flashed from one of the white figures, the other dropping to a knee. White streaks shot from the standing figure, tying the kneeling one by the wrists as it slowly approached. The black figure appeared to cry out, but its cries fell on deaf ears.

More figures appeared, these all gray. They danced circles around both the kneeling and the black figure, mocking them with their movements. The standing white figure closed in on the kneeling one, raising its sword and stabbing through it. It exploded into snowflakes before being blown across the fabric like a blizzard.

"Jaden?" Maya asked, but the weird vision didn't let me look away.

The van hit a pothole, sending all the figures tumbling to the ground. As it fell, the black figure, now unmistakably a woman among the tall, gray men, turned to cushion the fall for whatever she held. The scene was given an orange hue, and I was startled to see a face appear in the bright orange ball, which had grown to take up half the roof. The face belonged to a man, but not one I'd ever met. Chiseled cheekbones and a scarred forehead, with short black hair covering his head. He stared at me with fiery, dark blue eyes that glowed like mine. They tracked down back to the events unfolding below, where the black figure was surrounded, the white figure standing alongside the gray ones.

The gray men continued dancing before stopping, all looking at the black figure, who clutched a baby close to its chest. A brilliant flash of light, like a lightning bolt, struck down into the child, where it disappeared. The woman cried out before another flash encircled her. When the light vanished, the woman was gone, leaving only the lone white figure surrounded by the gray ones.

The white one glowed, clearly the leader among the others. Despite the poison, my brain worked, the pieces falling into place from what Maya had told me. My dad being killed, my mother sending me to Earth. I used the last of my strength to fight off the poison one last time. That made the white figure… Ian.

The face grinned at me as I made the connection.

"I'm sure you've heard many things, but I can assure you, I'm not who you think I am. Accept the offer, Jaden, and you can judge for yourself."

Ian's face melted away, replaced by a hooded man. Where his face should've been was a gray skull; its eyes hollow, endless pits.

"Join us, Maledictus," it said in a thin, raspy voice.

The skeleton extended his arm, stretching down from the ceiling, its bony hand covering my face, which burned like fire where the hand touched me. I could see the hood through the fingers, its constantly smiling face inches from mine. I stared into the black abyss of its eye sockets, fear gripping my chest, making it even harder to breathe.

"Join us," it hissed, as it launched forward.

The world went dark as I passed out.

Chapter Eight

My eyes flew open when I hit the ground. I'd been falling through the darkness, my stomach in my throat, as soon as I'd passed out. Shaking my legs, I tried to wake them up as I gathered my senses.

I sat on a field of grass. Tall stone walls ran the lengths of it, stretching out well beyond what I could see, as the field continued into the horizon. Figures stood erect on top of the stone hundreds of feet above me, watching as I climbed to my feet.

I'd no clue where I was, but nothing felt real. Like I was taking part in a lucid dream; aware it was imaginary, but a prisoner, trapped within the imagination. Memories of riding in the van came back, and something inside me told me this was still effects of the poison.

I watched the figures, scanning the tops of the walls as far away as I could, marveling at the number of them. They stared back, moving very little and making no noise. The wind whispered through the field, swaying the grass beneath me.

I was startled by the sudden appearance of a person just a few feet away from me. I tried to create my swords, but the ring was gone. The figure stood there, unmoving. More memories from the van came back, and I realized it was the same hooded skeleton I'd seen on the roof. A gray cloak covered its body, leaving only its face visible. The same dark, hollow eye sockets met thin cheekbones that stretched down to its jaw, trapped in the same constant, unnerving smile. The skeleton towered over me, at least a foot taller.

It raised its arm. Bony fingers stuck out of the cloak, motioning for me to follow as it turned and walked away from me. I followed it down a thin, matted-down path, as if this wasn't the first time the skeleton had led someone through this field. Flowers and taller crops grew off the path, growing more unkempt the farther away they got.

"Where are we going?" I asked.

"What are we doing?"

"Where are we?"

"Who are you?"

The skeleton answered each question with silence.

The figures on the walls watched us as we passed. They tracked us with turns of their heads and bodies, but they seemed rooted in place, unable to move on the wall.

Soon, people appeared in front of us. They were all couples, happy and smiling, dotting the sides of the path, paying us no attention. As we passed them, however, they crumbled into dust, blown away by the soft breeze. They were sparse at first, but quickly the sides of the path became populated by couples, each one joined by a third figure: Me.

Each family had a version of me, ranging from a young child to the teenager I was now. Some chatted around a dinner table while others embraced. One dad held me in his arms, spinning around like I was a plane. I laughed and laughed as I spun. Another mom smiled widely as I handed her a paper, ruffling my hair before hugging me tight. Each family differed from the others, but the one constant through all of them was me, and in each one I showed only overwhelming joy. We continued through them all, as if walking through a museum exhibit of all the other ways my life could've turned out.

They, too, crumbled as we passed. Each family blown away felt like a punch to the gut, and it took everything in me not to turn and run back the way I'd come. The hood in front of me marched onward, and I trudged behind it.

Others my age replaced the families. Again, they all changed, the one constant being me and my stupid smile. A group laughed in a library, covering their mouths when an angry librarian showed up to shush them. A boy and I played catch, talking without a care in the world as we threw the baseball. A girl and I lay close in the bed of a truck underneath a brilliant, starry night sky. I didn't recognize any of the others, but in each one I remained content before they were blown away as we passed.

After a few more scenes with friends, the mood of each scene changed. I watched myself in battle, each time fighting an unseen foe. I was never alone, fighting alongside others. Sometimes many, sometimes just a single person. Eventually, the battles faded, and a single scene played out on both sides of the path. A man and I stood, our backs together, swords readied for an attack. I instantly recognized the man. The face belonged to Ian, the same prominent features from the van standing out now. We passed the first showing of the battle. It crumbled into dust as the others began playing.

Ian and I fought, not against each other, but as a team. We fought invisible enemies, covering and helping the other one as if we'd been training our whole lives together. As we neared the last depiction, Ian stabbed through the air before turning to me. He stuck out a hand, shaking mine before wrapping an arm over my shoulders like a father might over their kid. The man had killed my dad, and I loathed him for it.

Families, friends, and Ian littered the sides of the path in front of me, each playing a different scenario. I refused to look at them, instead staring straight ahead with a clenched jaw. They, too, faded, leaving the skeleton and me alone on the path again.

Another scene played in the distance, too far away to make out any details, but coming into focus as we grew closer. My jaw muscles flexed in resentment as I realized what it was.

The skeleton stopped and held out his arm, forcing me to stand next to him and watch. The young couple who originally adopted me stood on the path, smiling and holding tight to a teenage boy, but this time it wasn't me.

The scene switched, and they played in a yard. A sprinkler sprayed in the air, and they took turns running through it and splashing each other as they enjoyed the cool water. I willed the water to freeze, but I had no effect on it. The vision changed again, and the dad sat in the passenger seat of the car, the boy in the driver's seat. The father, once my father, pointed to a parking spot where the boy easily navigated the car into it. They fist-bumped before exiting the car.

The boy and his mother appeared in the kitchen now, which was identical to how it was when I was that boy. My eyes welled up, and I turned to face the skeleton.

"Why are you showing me this?" I demanded.

It faced straight forward, not bothering to turn and acknowledge me or my question.

"Answer me!" I screamed at it.

Still, it did not reply, instead walking forward and through the scene, where the mom poured flour while the boy watched. I followed behind, the two crumbling to dust as my fist passed through the boy's face.

We continued through the field until a woman blocked the path. She looked to be in her early forties, and was lean, with long legs sticking out of a blue dress. Light brown hair matched her eyes, their sparkle unavoidable. She smiled warmly at me, and I smiled back, the anger and pain from the earlier visions melting away.

She held an arm out, and a young boy appeared. It wasn't me. Instead, Ollie wrapped his arms around her waist, squeezing tightly. She laughed, squeezing him back.

I moved closer, just feet away from my brother and the woman. She continued to smile at me, motioning with her free arm, inviting me closer. I moved toward her, close enough to be wrapped up by her arm.

I leaned in just as the skeleton appeared behind her, placing its fingers on her shoulder. Her smile faltered. A pained look crossed her face, the expression unlike anything I'd seen.

Ollie looked frightened, turning to me for help. I tried to

remove the skeleton's hand, but I was stuck in place, held back by some invisible force. Ollie and the woman began disintegrating, just as the others had. Cries of pain echoed off the enormous stone walls, though I'm not sure if they were from them or me. Slowly, they crumbled, taking a full five seconds to disappear.

The hood and I stared at each other. A stray tear ran down my face and I sniffed, waiting for the skeleton to say something... anything. After a few seconds, it too turned to dust, along with its counterparts on the walls all around, leaving me completely alone in the field. I closed my eyes as the gentle wind reclaimed the field as the only sound.

Chapter Nine

I opened my eyes, slowly this time, hoping the nightmare was over. To my relief, it was, but now light bombarded me through a dirty window. I drew in a big breath, rubbing my eyes as I swung my legs off the couch I was lying on, my bare feet hitting a carpeted floor. Bare feet? When did I take my shoes and socks off?

People moved around me, and I struggled to see them as I squinted through the beams of sun.

"Welcome back," a voice said, and I recognized it as Lucinda's, then seeing her to my right.

"Jaden!" Ollie wrapped me tight, burying his face in my arm.

"Hey, buddy," I said back, happy to see him not turned to dust. He let go, and the others joined around me.

"I thought you were going to die," Maya said.

"We couldn't get that lucky," Vincent replied, earning himself a punch in the arm.

I was no longer wearing my hoodie, instead a new t-shirt

that I'd never seen before. Someone changed my clothes while I was unconscious. I looked around, hoping to find the blue sweatshirt, not wanting to lose it. I found it on the couch behind me. It smelled clean and fresh, as if someone had washed it.

"Where are we?" I asked, putting the sweatshirt on.

"Indianapolis, amigo," Hugo answered, walking into the room with a glass of water.

"That's not Chicago." I accepted the glass from him. My throat burned as I drank, but soon the whole cup was gone. My stomach grumbled in response.

"No, it's not," Lucinda huffed.

The light gleamed through the windowsill, and a thought dawned on me. "Wait, what day is it?"

"Wednesday morning. You were out for the whole night," Maya said.

"And my van broke down," Hugo said. "But don't worry, Jadorino, cousin Matt will drive us there when he gets off work."

I nodded to him, then stood. My legs were a bit weak, but quickly regained strength. Other than being hungry, I felt surprisingly good for being poisoned only a day ago. I found my shoes near the front door of the house, my ankle socks tucked inside. After putting them on, I followed Hugo as he gave me a tour of the rest of the house. None of the others tagged along, probably receiving the same tour last night.

The house was nice. Hugo showed me the kitchen, walking me around the island, going as far as opening each drawer and making me a sandwich when I asked him. We toured the rest of the upstairs, passing back through the living room. I stopped, making eye contact with Maya in a *Help me* stare. But she just laughed as Hugo dragged me on, telling me to "Keep up, Jadorino."

Who told him my name?

We got to the basement. A punching bag hung from the ceiling in the center of the room, rubber mats layered the floor underneath it. Stray dumbbells littered areas around the punching bag, clearly Matt's attempt at a home gym. Hugo gave the bag a couple of jabs, laughing as he did. He told me to give it a try. I declined at first, but he was persistent, so I threw a few half-hearted punches. I could feel my Glacies power take control, predicting movement from the bag and counterattacks, despite the minimal effort. The ring dug painfully into my finger on my last punch, reminding me I was wearing it. I inspected it, but it hadn't changed.

Hugo showed me the rest of the basement, finishing with what he called "Me'n Matt's man cave."

It was nice, I admitted to him, before we returned to the living room.

Matt got off around 1:00, and it was midmorning when the tour finished. At first, we sat around, Hugo asking questions.

After the first couple received minimal answers, Lucinda said, "Hugo, as we told you when you asked about us the *entire* drive here and last night, we appreciate you taking us, but we would also appreciate it if you'd stop asking us questions. We just need to get to Chicago."

He was nice, but he was very curious about us, and I didn't blame him. After a couple more questions that weren't answered, he pointed at me.

"So, you, Jadorino. What was wrong with you yesterday? You were sick, but now you're fine. And why are your eyes glowing?"

I was about to blow this dude's mind.

But before I could, Lucinda stood up. "Sorry, Hugo, but I need to speak with him. Jaden, follow me, please."

I followed her out of the living room, through the kitchen, and into the garage.

"Let's try not to tell everyone you're Maledictus," she said, once the door was shut behind me.

"I didn't even say anything."

"I could tell you were about to."

"Didn't you say everyone would know?"

"In Arrortha, yes. Not here on Earth. Most Earth dwellers wouldn't believe you, even if you told them, anyway, so there's no point," she said, looking around the garage.

Tools lay on top of tables; shelves lined the walls with assorted items thrown haphazardly on them. Matt must've used this place as a shop, as engine and other car parts scattered among the tools.

Lucinda grabbed two thick bottles of motor oil from the shelf, placing them on the floor in the middle of the garage before coming up next to me.

"Make that ball of ice in your hand," she said, forming one herself.

I held out my hand, and the sphere of swirling ice formed and floated inches above it.

"You're left-handed?" she asked, narrowing her eyes.

"Yeah?"

"The phantom never predicted that. Anyway, that thing in your hand is what is lovingly referred to as a *viburnum*."

"A what?"

"You'd know it as a 'snowball.'"

"Fitting."

"It is. Now, I want you to shoot it at one of these bottles."

She faced one of the bottles on the floor, turning her hand toward it. The *viburnum* raced from her hand, shooting across the garage at the bottle, where it slammed into it with a thwack, and covered it with a thick layer of ice.

I focused on the other bottle, extending my arm and turning my hand just as she did. The ball shot out of my hand, chilling the air around it. The second bottle got covered in ice, just like the first.

She nodded approval, then swiped her hand in front of her, removing the ice from the bottle.

I did the same, the ice from my bottle disappearing as well. My eyebrows shot up in surprise, leading to a chuckle from Lucinda.

"Not bad, kid. As you've discovered, the ice is at your command."

We practiced a few more times on stationary bottles before Lucinda started tossing them in the air, forcing me to freeze them mid-air. I missed the first few times, leading to the snowballs freezing different parts of the garage door. With practice, however, I was able to hit the bottle in the air, even when Lucinda made me turn around after she had already thrown it.

Next it was on to shields. "A Glacies must be able to use their powers for offense and defense," she said. "Yes, you can dodge, but sometimes it is better to block."

Lucinda is a big believer in the "trial and error" method of teaching, because soon empty jugs and assorted tools were flying at me. I ducked under the first few, wondering what was wrong with this woman.

"No ducking! Block!" she'd yell, then throw another empty bottle at me.

I narrowly dodged an oil filter I have no idea where she found. "Trust yourself, Jaden. Control your powers. It's the only way you'll stay alive." She readied another bottle. She arced this one, giving me time to watch as it neared. I brought my hand up to meet it, creating a wall of ice in front of it. The bottle clanked off the ice, falling harmlessly to the floor as the ice disappeared as quickly as it had formed.

"That's it!" she declared, already grabbing another bottle.

She worked her way around, grabbing and throwing bottles off the ground rapidly, forcing me to adjust and create different shields for each one, sometimes using my left, sometimes my right, and, occasionally, both hands. She reached a full circle, still throwing assorted items, which began to pile at my feet. Finally, she grabbed a wheeled toolbox, pushing it at me with all her might.

With no hesitation, I brought my left foot forward, swinging my arms down in an arc. Ice poured out from each hand, creating a thick barrier that stretched the width of the garage. The toolbox slammed into the wall, which didn't budge. Tools rattled and fell, clanking inside the toolbox. Above all, I could hear Lucinda shouting cries of praise, her student successfully passing her latest test.

I didn't have time to celebrate with her, as a sharp twinge gripped the middle of my chest. Pain grew and shrank with each breath, and clouds of frozen vapor escaped with each exhale. I bent over, exhausted and hurting.

"What's happening?" I asked weakly. My teeth chattered and my whole body shivered.

"This is the curse of Glacies," she said calmly. "It'll pass. You just need to rest."

She guided me to the steps leading into the house, where she sat next to me, draping her cloak over me for extra warmth. "Your heart is freezing from the inside," she explained. "It is the way Glacies are prevented from overusing their powers."

We sat in silence for a few minutes. Eventually, my breath returned to warm air, and the pain in my heart lessened to only a slight throb with each beat.

"Why are you teaching me this stuff now?" I asked her. "Why not wait until we get back?"

Lucinda looked at the bottles on the floor, taking her time before answering.

"Because it may not be much safer for you there than it is here."

"Maya told me that's because of Ian."

She nodded. "I'm sure she's told you about my past then. The main reason I was considering Ian to rule Highmoore was his ability to… influence people, and at one point, I thought the same way as him. But then I didn't choose him, and now he's causing turmoil among the people, using that ability."

"What do you mean?"

"Look at it this way: There are multiple kingdoms, cities, whatever you want to call them, in Arrortha. They've had their disagreements, sure, but for as long as I've been alive, they've worked well enough with each other as one, even if it was done out of fear. But now, Ian has convinced entire kingdoms that Highmoore, and you specifically, are a threat to their existence. There are even people in Highmoore who agree with him."

"Maya said he wants me to join him. Why is he telling everyone I'm a threat if he wants me to join him?"

"He knows you two would be nearly impossible to defeat, but if you side with your mother, he wants as many people against you as possible."

I didn't respond, instead absorbing what she told me. I'd never met her, but just the opportunity to meet and live with my real mom was driving me forward now, and I couldn't see how I'd ever side with Ian. I'd kept the dream to myself, not wanting to explain what I'd seen, since I wasn't sure myself.

Next to me, Lucinda slapped her knees and stood, taking her cloak back.

"But Maledictus, that is why I am teaching you now, because there will be others who want to kidnap you, or worse, from the moment we get there. I think you'll present more of a challenge than they're bargaining for," she said with a wink. "Go find Vinny. Tell him I told you to train with him until it's time to go."

I sighed, stood, and headed for the door into the house.

"And Jaden," she called, "do listen to him. I know you two aren't best friends, but he is able to teach you a lot."

Five minutes later, Vincent and I stood on the rubber mats on either side of the punching bag in the basement, each of us holding a length of PVC pipe we had found propped up against a nearby wall. Maya sat on a couch, watching the lesson.

"There are three forms of attacks," he said. "Thrusts, slashes, and cuts." He showed each one, starting with a thrust, which was a forward, stabbing motion. For a slash, he brought the pipe across the punching bag, hitting it in the side. He arced the pipe high over his head, swinging down and hitting the punching bag on the top for a cut.

"You may not have known the names for all of those before, but your Glacies power knew how to do each. Moving forward, it's about unlocking each one and using it correctly, which will help you reach your full potential. You're only going to learn that through experience, so let's get to it. Show me your stance," he said, poking my chest with the PVC pipe.

I brought the pipe up, using my left foot to lead.

"A lefty? That's interesting. Open your stance a little and angle your body more. Like this."

I matched his stance, positioning myself like he did. "Good, I want you to mirror my movements."

He went slowly through each attack, speeding up as we practiced them a third and fourth time. By the fifth time, I was leading while he mirrored my movements.

"You're not the worst I've ever seen."

It was as close to a compliment as I was going to get from him.

"Let's get a little more dangerous. You attack, I'll defend. For now, I won't do any counter attacks, so get creative. Never let me know your next move."

"I won't let you know my first move," I said. Admittedly, it sounded a lot cooler in my head.

I leapt to the side, bringing the pipe up to match his. I feigned a simple thrust, knocking away his pipe with a more powerful strike, my attack ending with a slash when he was defenseless.

At least, that was the plan. However, when I landed, my foot caught under a stray dumbbell, preventing me from shifting my weight to thrust the pipe forward. Instead, I fell awkwardly, crashing onto other sets of dumbbells, which didn't break my fall.

Vincent soon loomed over me. "You're right. I did not know you were going to do that."

I looked back at Maya, who covered her mouth with her hand, doing her best to avoid eye contact and bust out into laughter. I stood up fast, my face red with embarrassment.

"Let's pretend that didn't happen," I said, wielding the PVC again.

Vincent laughed across from me, but he too leveled his weapon.

I tried straight attacks, trying to combo them together to throw Vincent off balance, but he blocked each one with ease. On one attack, I spun when the pipes collided. He wasn't prepared for this, but jumped back just far enough to avoid the end of the pipe when I lunged at him.

I stepped back. "This isn't helping. I need you to fight back."

Vincent smiled. "As you wish, Maledictus." He closed the distance between us, feigning an attack with his right before switching hands and swinging with his left. I blocked it, turning the pipe over in my hand to block a second attack aimed at my left shoulder.

He kept trying different attacks, but my sixth sense had taken over. I would parry them, following with my own attacks. Soon I was finding gaps in Vincent's defenses. I hit him in the arm, shoulder, and ribs, the PVC pipe flying around faster than he could react. He grew more and more frustrated, sweat beating down his brow as he tried to counterattack.

He grazed my lower leg, swiping to the side after I'd deflected his pipe down. I blocked his following attack, frustrated for slipping up. We were both exhausted, neither of us willing to give up first. As he prepared for his next attack, I switched the pipe to my right hand, trying something I'd obviously never done before.

He swung diagonally. I brought my pipe up to meet his, the two connecting at head height. I stepped closer, letting my PVC pipe flatten. Vincent's slid down the length of mine, falling toward the ground once the two lost contact. As this happened, I brought my arm around his weapon, pointing mine straight down, trapping his between my arm and my side. With him not able to move, I ran my arm inside of his, the PVC pipe against his inner forearm. I swung my hips, pushing the opposite way against his elbow. His grip loosened and eventually let go. I spun in one motion, now on his side. My left hand held his weapon, now pointed at the back of his neck. My right hand held mine, laid across his throat, preventing him from moving.

We both breathed heavily.

He side-eyed me angrily before removing the PVC pressed against his throat. He turned, his demeanor suddenly calm, a smile creeping across his face. "Not bad," he said, patting me on the back.

I tensed up with the contact.

Maya appeared on the stairs carrying two bottles of water. "What did I miss?" she asked, handing each of us one.

"We called it a draw," I said.

"No way," Vincent said with a laugh. "He killed me."

* * *

We sat on the rubber mats, taking sips of water. My side ached dully, but it seemed to have gotten better. I wondered if Maya had healed the cut again when she was taking the poison.

I listened as Maya and Vincent made small talk. They talked freely, chatting about their training sessions back in Arrortha, Maya's lessons with someone named Jane, who I deciphered was some popular teacher, and Vincent's adventures with others he called "junior *Venators,*" or hunters. They laughed and exchanged stories like old friends. Every so often, and usually during the best parts of the story, Maya would lean over and touch his shoulder or put her hand on his knee, looking genuinely interested in his stories. I tried to focus on them, trying to get an understanding of what my home would be like, but too many of his tales featured places I didn't know or people I'd never met, and soon I tuned them out, instead looking at the rest of the basement.

The mention of my name drew me back in.

"What do you think Jaden would be back home?" Maya asked him.

"Hmm," Vincent said, pretending to be deep in thought. "As he is now?"

"Yes."

"He's a hunter or a searcher, too talented not to be. Although, that's assuming he isn't castle-bound right away. He is still the queen's son."

Maya cocked her head, trying to envision me as whatever those things Vincent had said. "He's got the skills to be a hunter, but I don't see it. Searcher seems better, but he's first in line for the throne. I don't think Queen Iris lets him leave the castle."

"Hey, do either of you want to explain anything about what you're saying?" I asked, annoyed the topic had made its way to me.

"Right! Searchers are what we call do-it-alls. You want information, you find a searcher. You want someone to go buy a pig because you're too lazy, call a searcher. They live an interesting life, though mundane compared to a Venator—a hunter," Vincent said. Without me asking, he continued explaining. "A hunter can either be part of Highmoore's army or work directly for the queen."

"What do they hunt for?"

"Usually enemies of the queen. Sometimes not."

"And what do they do when they find who they're looking for?"

"Depends on what the queen asks them to do. Don't worry, it's become a lot more 'search and rescue' since your mother took power. She's a Medela, so she's not as aggressive as certain past queens."

"And you're a hunter?"

"A junior hunter," Maya corrected, laughing when Vincent gave her a dirty look.

"They don't allow you to become a true hunter until you turn twenty," Vincent said.

"How old are you?"

"Nineteen. When we get back, I will have a couple months before I'm official. You'd have some time before you could join, but I know you'd be accepted quickly."

Maya stood, grabbing the PVC pipe lying next to me. "You picked up a sword for the first time, I'm assuming, two days ago, and you've already won more actual fights than Vinny here has."

Vincent rolled his eyes. "Don't make me tell Queen Iris to put you on her bad list. Not like it would do anything, though."

"She would never, and you know it."

"Of course, you'll have to avoid Ian's Venators," Vincent said, turning back to me. "They'll be hunting you as soon as you step foot in Arrortha."

"Stop trying to scare him. He's already got enough to worry about," Maya said to him before turning to me as well. "You'll be well protected, and from what I've seen, able to fend for yourself."

"He's more than capable, M." Vincent stood, giving me a fist bump before heading for the stairs. "Maybe I can practice with you when we get back. I could learn a thing or two," he said as he climbed.

He disappeared upstairs, leaving Maya and me alone in the basement.

"See, he's not that bad."

Sometimes.

I half-smiled in response, trying to muster the energy to drag my aching body off the floor. Instead of helping, Maya sat cross-legged opposite me. I gave up the effort to stand, instead lying down, propping myself up on my elbows to see her.

"How long have you guys known each other?" I asked. I wanted to keep the conversation off me, but I was also curious, seeing the way she interacted with him.

"A while now. I'd recently gotten my Medela powers and was

training with some others. He was well into the Venator program but had gotten a nasty cut during training. He was my first successful heal, though it wasn't easy. I was so nervous, I kept messing up. After two fails, they wanted to have someone else try, but he wouldn't let anyone else do it."

"Why?"

"He kept telling them he wanted me to do it, to show myself I was capable, that I just had to trust myself. When I finally healed his cut, he looked… proud, like he knew I could do it. We became friends after that, and he's kind of evolved into a brother to me. Sure, he can get annoying, but he is always telling me I'm strong, and he pushes me to be the best I can be."

"Oh. Cool."

"Yeah. Say, I've been meaning to ask you. You mumbled a lot while you were passed out. Did you have any dreams or visions while you were passed out?"

The families and the skeleton came flooding back. How could she possibly know about that? No, I figured, she had to be guessing. "Not really."

She studied my face. I did my best not to look guilty, but I could tell I wasn't great at it.

"So… yes, then. What did you see?"

I hadn't yet decided what I'd seen.

"I don't want to talk about it," I said, hoping I didn't sound too snotty.

"That's fine. If you want to sometime, just bring it up."

"Okay."

We sat in silence for a few seconds before she stood. "I'm going to head upstairs. Hugo's cousin should be home soon, and we're hopefully leaving soon after."

I nodded awkwardly, but didn't say anything as she disappeared up the stairs.

I let myself lie flat on my back and stare up at the ceiling. Groaning, I cussed at myself under my breath. I had no idea how to talk to girls my age.

Matt got home thirty minutes later. Hugo had told him about us, but still, he eyed each of us with amused suspicion as he entered the house.

"You said a couple people, Hugo," he said, hanging a bag on the back of the door and kicking his shoes off.

"This is a couple."

"This is five. I have five total seats in my car."

"There are a couple smaller ones that could probably fit in the trunk," Hugo said, motioning to Ollie and me. I gave him a *Dude, really?* look, but he just smiled at me.

"Don't worry, Jadorino, it'll only be a couple of hours."

Matt sighed. "Whatever. I'm going to change and make a sandwich. Then we will leave."

Hugo gave him a salute, a goofy grin plastered across his face. Matt rolled his eyes as he passed on his way to the bedroom.

"Don't worry about him. He was in the army, takes things too seriously now. You know how it goes," Hugo said, the grin still resting on his face. If he picked up on the fact that none of his five guests "knew how it goes," he didn't show it.

* * *

Matt had his sandwich made and half eaten ten minutes later. He had changed from his red work polo to a simple gray t-shirt and jeans. His short-cropped hair was gelled into spikes which held firm in the early afternoon breeze, contrasting Hugo's freely blowing mullet. Before we got to the car, Matt made Lucinda show him the three hundred dollars she promised to take us. Honestly, I didn't blame him.

He opened the trunk of his old-looking Dodge Challenger, and with a bored look, waved to Ollie and me to get in. Ollie climbed in without a word. I locked eyes with Matt before entering, looking to see if he'd give away he was actually a Desolate.

He just glared back, the same bored look on his face. "Don't worry, I'll drive smoothly."

I wasn't thrilled about it, but I climbed in the back. The trunk closed behind me, and Ollie and I were plunged into darkness.

The darkness and the car rocking on the road threatened to lull me to sleep an hour later. I forced myself to stay awake, afraid of what I'd dream if I did fall asleep. Ollie had been quiet for most of the ride, outside of the occasional yawn or whimper. I could feel his hand resting between my shoulder blades, making sure I didn't go anywhere and leave him alone in the darkness.

Muffled conversation made its way through the back seat. It was hard to distinguish voices, but it sounded to be mainly from Hugo, who had refused to stay behind, and Vincent. I thought I heard my name twice, but I couldn't be certain.

Behind me, Ollie stretched, his tiny figure able to extend full despite being in a trunk. I was stuck near the fetal position, and jealous.

After a yawn, he said, "I miss home."

I don't.

I hadn't considered it home when I lived there. As far as I was concerned, I've never had a true home. I racked my brain, looking for anything to say to him. I settled on, "We're going to a new home. Hopefully, one we will like better."

"I don't want to. I liked that one," he said, pushing against my back. "Are Mom and Dad even coming? You said they were!"

I sighed. "No, Ollie, they aren't. I'm sorry."

He retreated as far as he could into the trunk away from me. The sounds of the road filled the void. Soon, I heard soft sniffles from deep in the darkness.

I struggled, looking for words that I knew wouldn't come. We were different people. He longed for the comfort brought to him by those in his life now. I refused to look back, instead clinging to the small hope I *was* the son of a woman I'd never met, from a world I didn't know existed, and that, just maybe, there was a place where I wouldn't be thrown aside like expired leftovers. I felt bad for Ollie. He had finally found a home he loved, and I was ripping him away from it. I would protect him for as long as I was still breathing, but there was no going back.

"Jaden?" Ollie's voice, weak and scared, called to me.

"Yeah, buddy?"

"When we get to this new home, are you going to be famous?"

"I sure hope not. I know nothing about where we're going."

"If you are famous there, are you going to leave me?"

I felt a physical pain in my heart. I understood the question: Was I going to be like everyone else in his life?

"Never. You're stuck with me until the end."

He scooted closer, angling himself so his head rested in my mid-back, where his hand had been earlier.

"I think I'm okay with that."

Chapter Ten

The car rolled to a stop sometime later. Doors opened and closed, followed by footsteps making their way toward the back of the vehicle. The trunk didn't open right away, but when it did, light flooded the once-dark capsule. I pulled my hood over my head as I dragged my cramping legs out of the trunk and onto the pavement below.

"Dude, it's eighty-five degrees," Vincent said.

"It's the sun. It's bright as—"

"I'm going to miss you, Jadorino!" Hugo said, climbing out of the car last. He walked toward me, arms out, looking for anyone who would hug him back. I looked at Matt, who shook his head and rolled his eyes as he made his way back to the driver's seat without a word.

Hugo reached me, wrapping his arms around tightly. The ring vibrated on my finger, ready to create a weapon to get this guy off me. I forced it not to, instead waiting awkwardly for him to release me.

He finally did, drawing back to look at me like a proud father would look at his son when dropping him off for college. In a shaky voice, he said one last "Goodbye, everyone. Goodbye, Jadorino," before turning with one final sniff and getting in the car.

Lucinda grabbed my wrist as they drove off, dragging me toward the train station in front of us. I shook her off and walked on my own. I was getting tired of people touching me.

In front of us was the third Union station I'd been to in the last three days. Maybe I should've collected postcards from each. I could've mailed them back to Rose once we got to Denver. *Hey, your son isn't actually from Earth. Have a nice life!*

But as we entered the station, I continued past the gift store, putting my old life behind me. People crowded around us as we walked deeper into the station. Evening rush hour was just starting, and passengers flooded off and onto trains and buses, waited in rows of chairs, or milled about looking for a snack or an interesting way to pass the time.

We found the ticket counter well into the station: a cavernous room with arched ceilings made of stained glass. Rows of benches, all occupied, filled most of the room. The voices of travelers echoed around, making it hard to think, and much harder to hear. I led us to the ticket line where we waited for others to buy their tickets. Ollie hung close to me, nervous with the sheer number of people in the room.

After a long wait, during which Lucinda eyed each person carefully, it was our turn to buy tickets.

"Welcome to Union Station," said the older woman behind the counter. "What can I help you with?"

"When is your next train to Denver?" I asked.

"Thirty minutes from now. At least, it was supposed to be. It's not running tonight. I was told someone messed with the track in Denver."

Lucinda shook her head. "Ian's men. We aren't supposed to harm Earth dwellers or effect anything on Earth, but he will do whatever it takes to stop you."

The lady behind the counter shrugged her shoulders as if it was just another day. "What can you do?" She told us it wouldn't run until the morning, as they were going to fix the track overnight. "Here's this," she said, handing over a piece of paper. "It's a hotel voucher. Just bring it back in the morning and you can get your tickets. Train leaves at seven-forty a.m., so be here early!"

I thanked her, then followed the rest of the group back through the crowded station and onto the street.

It took us fifteen minutes to walk to the hotel provided by the station. Actually, hotel was a strong word for it. The two-story building was nestled between two office buildings that rose high into the sky, its old-looking brick contrasting the modern glass and marble of its surroundings.

Musky, smoky air seemed to press down on the low light, making the inside feel claustrophobic. Old furniture lined the windows, looking out into the street.

"At least it was free," I muttered to Maya as I walked up to the front desk.

"Station stray?" the man behind the counter asked.

"Huh?"

"The paper. I'm assuming it's from the station. They love to put groups like yours up here." He sighed. "Let me see it."

I handed it to him and waited while he typed on his computer. After multiple clicks, he handed the paper back to me, along with a couple of keycards.

"The station must've been feeling generous today; they gave you two rooms. You'll be in two fourteen and two sixteen. The elevator is here in the lobby, but it's out of service. Stairs are at the end of the hall. Enjoy your stay with us."

I'm sure I wasn't going to.

The lobby was empty except for us and the guy behind the counter, who now scrolled on his phone, blowing bubbles with his chewing gum. We passed the elevator, looking over the caution tape and into the open shaft.

"Out of service!" came a yell from the front.

We found our first room on the second floor. The door swung open to reveal a pair of queen-sized beds in the center of a quiet, dank room. A single bedside table sat next to each bed, while a couple of desks with moldy legs sat on either side of a small TV.

"Make yourselves comfortable," Lucinda said. "Maya and I will be back soon."

They headed off to the second room while Ollie, Vincent, and I stayed. None of us had much that we were traveling with, so it didn't take long for the three of us to settle into the room. Ollie and I sat on a bed, flipping through the channels we could get on the TV. We ended on a History Channel documentary about the planets. It didn't interest me all that much, but Ollie grabbed the remote and refused to change it, so I half watched and half thought about which planet Arrortha might be on; I didn't understand the whole "different realm" thing yet.

Vincent had grabbed a rolling chair from one of the desks and now sat looking out over as much of the Chicago skyline as the second-story window would allow. The sun glinted off the side of his face, his green eyes shining bright. He looked to be deep in thought, his face twisting and squinting as if he was in the middle of an argument with someone. I watched him for a while until he noticed. He nodded at me but went right back to looking out the window.

Maya and Lucinda knocked on the door twenty minutes later. "Maledictus," Maya said.

"You can just say Jaden."

"Okay. Jaden, there's something I want to show you."

"Hopefully food?"

"We can pick something up on the way if you need to. It's not that far from here."

"Is it something related to Arrortha?" I asked.

She nodded in reply.

"Can he go?" I motioned toward Ollie.

Lucinda shook her head. "It's best if he didn't. You two will be quick, and then we can all go eat." She looked at the clock on the nightstand. It wasn't yet six. "You guys will be gone no longer than an hour," she said, eyeing Maya.

"Shouldn't be. It'll be a quick history lesson today. Let's go."

I stood reluctantly to follow, looking back at Ollie, who was still glued to the planets.

"Go. He will be fine," Lucinda said.

I followed Maya out of the room. "I'd rather learn how to fight than more history," I said.

"You already know how to do that. Plus, if I'm going to get you back alive and be your friend, I can't have you being cursed, powerful, *and* dumb."

* * *

Maya and I piled into a taxi minutes later. She handed an address scribbled on a small piece of paper to the driver, who took it with a grunt, started his meter, and pulled out into the street.

Buildings crawled by as the taxi trudged through near stand-still traffic. I asked Maya where we were going, but all she would tell me was that she was going to show me another power I had, which only made me more anxious.

Though I don't think we went very far, it took us more than twenty minutes before the taxi pulled to the side of the street. Maya paid the fare as we exited the taxi, coaxing me to hurry up. I made eye contact with the driver through the rearview mirror. He looked amused at the scene in his backseat but peeled away as soon as the door shut.

I stood next to Maya in front of a stadium. Tan stones made up the outside wall, covered by red shingle awnings. Green railings ran the length of the stadium with flags and signs hung across the edges, advertising different gates and sponsors. A mammoth, bright-red scoreboard towered above the main gate, welcoming everyone to Wrigley Field: Home of The Chicago Cubs.

"Why are we at a baseball stadium?" I asked, looking at her.

She didn't make eye contact, instead scanning the front for a way in. "Is that what this is? Did you play here?"

"Only in my dreams," I muttered. "What does this have to do with Arrortha?"

"I'll show you. Follow me."

We searched around the outside, looking for some way into the stadium, as there was clearly no game tonight. The sun was just beginning to set when we spotted an open maintenance gate. We sat on the edge of a large planter, watching a few people wheel bottles of soda out of the back of a truck.

When their carts were all loaded, they disappeared into the stadium, Maya standing to follow them. I was close behind her, doing my best to look as natural as she did as she entered the open gate and headed in the opposite direction the workers had gone.

The stadium lights were dim as we snuck through the concourse. Outside of the truck unloaders, we didn't run into anyone else.

I followed Maya down an aisle, reaching the field just past the third base dugout. She slipped between a gap in the netting that ascended from the top of the dugout, landing gracefully in the camera well. I shimmied my way under the net as well, surprising myself by landing softly next to her. After a brief look around, Maya led us out into the outfield and all the way to the wall that separated the stands from the field.

"Here we are," Maya said, looking up at the tall wall in front of us.

"We snuck into this place so you could show me a wall?"

"Not *the* wall. What's on the wall."

I walked up closer, reaching out to touch the green plants that covered the entire structure. "Ivy?"

The ivy moved around my hand as I touched it. It felt alive, wrapping around my wrist, pulling gently.

"*Hedera*, yes. How do you think it got here?"

"I'm going to guess it was planted."

"Sort of. An old Crescere placed it here, long ago. A man by the name of Clifton Lewis."

"I don't know why I was expected to know that," I said, removing my hand from the ivy, which returned to pressing up against the wall. Maya took my place, but the ivy had no interest in her.

"The point is, Jaden, Crescere is another power you have. It means 'to grow.' Trees, crops, ivy. If it's a plant, you can make it grow."

"The entire power is making plants grow?"

"You say that like it's a bad thing, but it sure makes feeding everyone a lot easier. Vines and ivy are climbing tools as well."

"What's the catch then?"

"What do you mean?"

"You said each power has its own curse. Glacies is freezing my heart, but what is this one?" I asked.

"Don't do it, but you could swipe your hand, and all of this ivy would disappear."

I stared blankly at her.

She seemed frustrated that I wasn't getting it. "Anybody with the Crescere power can control any plant, even if it was created by a different person. According to Lewis' own book, this ivy was put here and has thrived for almost ninety years. Any Crescere, even a brand new twelve-year-old, who has never once practiced, could come and wipe it away without a second thought."

"So its curse is trust? Trust that others won't sabotage you?"

"That's one way to look at it. Ian has been sending multiple Crescere to wipe away crops for the last few years. It is also the most common power, so there is never a shortage of suspects. So much so that the few community gardens we have left are guarded."

"Can they not just sprout an apple and eat it before anyone notices?"

"It takes a long time to master the power to that point. Most Cresceres aren't that skilled, even with decades of practice."

I digested everything she was telling me. I could control plants, as long as there wasn't anyone around who didn't want me to. Based on what I'd been told so far, many people would not want me living, much less growing vegetation. On the bright side, my plant getting bigger in biology class a few days ago made much more sense.

"Why hasn't this ivy been removed by the people of Earth?" I asked, running my hand back through the ivy, mesmerized as each leaf swayed toward me, as if my hand were a magnet. "It seems like a hazard on a baseball field."

"In short, they can't. It'll just come back way quicker than they can get rid of it. Any Crescere can remove it, but a non-Crescere can't. Plus, I think they like it."

"Well, they kind of have to," I mumbled.

I decided to try out the power, hoping I didn't accidentally remove it. With my hand still in the ivy, I focused on making more. A thick canopy of green leaves sprouted from the wall. Everywhere I moved my hand, more leaves appeared.

Maya smiled approvingly as I walked through the dirt between the fence and the grass in the outfield, adding more ivy to the already covered brick wall. I made it to centerfield, following the dirt track, passing the number "400" painted in bright yellow directly onto the brick.

"Don't touch the ivy!" a voice yelled from somewhere in the stadium. My head whipped around as a police officer sprinted toward us. He said something into his radio before yelling at us to stay where we were.

Maya and I, being teenagers caught somewhere we weren't supposed to be, did the exact opposite.

The officer was almost halfway through the outfield. Taller walls on the sides of the field limited our escape routes, leaving the ivy-covered wall in front of us as our only way to escape.

I took one stride before leaping as high onto the wall as I could, grabbing hold of the ivy, which gripped my hands and wrists just as hard back. I reached for fistfuls of the plant as it helped to push my feet up as I climbed. Near the top, I checked back on Maya, who was climbing much slower, seeming to tangle in the ivy more and more as she attempted to climb.

"Help her," I ordered the ivy, not sure if that was how the power worked. On command, the foliage began to assist her in climbing just as it was helping me.

I reached the top of the wall, where I ran into my next problem. A net basket ran the entire length of the wall, jutting out a few feet over my head. To get past it, I would have to jump backward, grab the wire that the net connected to, and pull myself over it. I figured I was strong enough to do it, plus I could freeze my hand to the net in case I started to fall. With the assistance of the ivy, I considered it doable.

I grabbed as much ivy as I could, brought my legs up close to my chest, and thrust off the wall at an angle, the ivy giving me a boost (as much as a plant could) as I pushed off. My eyes stayed glued to the wire. My hands, already partially frozen, reached out, connecting with and freezing to it, stopping the momentum of the rest of my body. With an insane amount of adrenaline, I pulled myself up, tumbling down into the basket.

There was no time to celebrate, as the cop neared the dirt and Maya, who had reached the top of the wall, was just now realizing the problem she faced.

"How did you get up there?" she asked frantically, looking at me through the mesh of the net.

"I jumped. Push off the wall and grab my hand," I said, leaning my upper half over the edge of the basket. "The ivy will help you."

"Don't drop me."

"Then don't miss."

She jumped off the wall, the ivy boosting her. Her hand clasped around my wrist; my hand doing the same to hers. I used my weight to pull her up, tumbling backward into the basket as she helped to pull herself above the wire, rolling down the net, landing on top of me. The pain in my side flared and I got a mouthful of hair as we became entangled.

We both jumped to our feet, scrambling over rows of seats as we continued our escape. Back below us, the cop yelled into his radio, telling his partners that we had made it into the stands and were still running.

We ran in front of a giant scoreboard, our footfalls echoing throughout the empty stadium. Radio squawks and shouts grew in volume around us as concession stands raced by us. The workers we had seen unloading the truck earlier watched with amused smiles as we passed them on the concourse. Maya gave them a half-wave, which was met with a chorus of laughs and a "Better run!"

Maybe it was the adrenaline, or maybe it was the way sunlight glinted off her tan skin. Either way, feelings I'd never felt before ran inside me just as fast as I was next to her. I tried to push them aside and focus on our escape, but it was difficult to do.

We were headed back toward the unlocked gate, hoping to sneak out before we were found again. We hadn't made it halfway there when we came face to face with a trio of cops blocking the concourse and our escape plan.

Maya pushed me left down a hallway that led into the inner workings of the stadium while she went right, back into the seating area. All three cops turned to chase, following me down an eerily dim concrete tunnel. I looked behind me, but Maya continued, slipping away into the seats. Once again, I was on my own. Gone were the feelings I had moments ago, instead replaced by different thoughts.

I'll show her. I don't need her help to get away.

I followed the tunnel for a while, taking a series of turns, scanning signs as I ran, hoping one would lead me back to ground level. I ran as fast as my fit legs would allow, but slowly and surely, the cops gained ground behind me.

Finally, I found it. A sign in the shape of an arrow, pointing in the direction of the concourse. I turned and sprinted down the hall, pumping my legs as fast as they would go. I skidded around the corner and into the middle of the open concourse. After taking a brief moment to look around, I saw I was near the gate we'd entered. I took off in that direction, the thumping of the cop's boots not even twenty feet behind me.

The late evening sun shone onto the smooth pavement outside of Wrigley Field. I rounded a corner, heading for the open gate and eventual freedom, but the gate was open no more. Well, technically, it was still open. However, no less than six cops stood in a line, blocking any chance of riding off into the setting sun. They neared as a unit while the three cops chasing me closed the backside, trapping me inside their circle.

I surveyed each cop, spinning slowly as I realized the dire situation I was in. A few held their hands by their waists, but most were out in front of them, pleading with me to not try anything stupid.

"Put your hands up and lay flat on the ground," one of the cops said as they inched closer, slimming the circle.

The ring buzzed wildly, demanding I choose a weapon and protect myself. I ignored it, unmoving, my eyes taking on a thousand-yard stare, fixated on nothing but the blurred horizon in front of me.

I'd given up on life this time. I wanted to fight. Not in an effort to escape, but in hopes of losing everything I could. Yet I remained still, my mind and body numb.

I vaguely heard a "Kid, you all right?" through the static that filled my ears. I registered a single cop reach me, grab me roughly around the arm, and twist it around my back toward the other one. I was forced to my knees as my wrists were cuffed together. Throughout it all, Ollie was the only thought I could muster. My life would be simple. I might get a light sentence for trespassing, then get sent back to the Edwards, who may or may not accept me. They'd question me about Ollie but wouldn't believe what I told them. Worst case, I'd end up in another foster home. At fifteen the odds of me being placed again were slim. No, I'd live there a few years, get kicked out at eighteen, then live the rest of my miserable life somewhere else until some of Ian's guys found me.

But Ollie. I'd failed the only person I cared about. What would his life be like? Would Lucinda take him back to Arrortha with her, or would they dump him on the side of the street? After all, I was the one they wanted, not him.

I was dragged to my feet and marched out to the street, a cop on either side of me. I was placed on the curb in between two police cars as a mass of cops gathered around.

Inside, I stewed. Maya entered and left my mind, just as she had my life. I'd only been this mad at three people in my life: my adoptive mom and dad when they abandoned me, and now her. Like a breeze, she was gone at the first true test. *See ya, Jaden. Good luck not getting caught.* I couldn't believe I'd thought she was different.

"What's your name?" one of the cops asked, holding a notepad and a pen.

"Jaden Frost," I answered, staring straight ahead.

"What are you doing in the stadium, Jaden?"

"Trusting people I shouldn't."

The cop seemed to think it over, chuckling at the response. "At least you've realized that. My officers tell me you were with a girl. Who was she?"

In my mind, it didn't matter. They wouldn't find her anyway, so I said nothing. The officer repeated the question, again getting no response from me. He asked a few more questions, like where I lived, what my parents' names were, if the girl was my sister or not. I'd lost interest again, so I answered him with silence. He flipped the notepad shut, returning to his car, where he closed the door and began typing on his computer. The other cops stood around. I noticed them occasionally stealing glances and whispering among themselves, but I couldn't hear any of the conversations.

Ten minutes passed, and the cop had yet to return. In those ten minutes, I'd become resolute that I would do whatever I could to make sure Ollie was safe. Scanning the surrounding area, I looked for places where I could potentially go if I could get away from these cops. As I followed the sidewalk across the street, a familiar-looking girl with brown hair materialized out of the shadows of a building, staring directly at me.

I looked at the ground, cursing my mind for its hallucinations. Squeezing my eyes shut, I looked back, expecting the street to be empty. But Maya was still there, now moving her body in what I can only describe as an interpretive dance.

I shook my head in disgust, looking back at the ground. Was she back here to mock me? *Some Maledictus. Couldn't even get away from human cops.* I refused to look at her. Ten seconds, twenty. Finally, thirty seconds later, I looked back across the street. She was still there, but her stare had turned into a glare. Even from my distance, I could tell she was pleading with me, her eyes yelling *Please, Jaden, look at me.*

I was still unbelievably mad at her, but she was my best chance at getting away. When she was sure I was paying attention, she turned, putting her hands behind her back. From behind her, she made an expanding motion with her hands, separating her arms as if she had freed herself from the invisible handcuffs. She turned around to see if I'd understood. My expression gave it away, and her shoulders slumped as her head tilted, showing her annoyance. She changed her tactics as we played charades from across the street.

She pointed toward me, then to herself. With her right hand, she imitated creating a viburnum. She "shot" it at her left hand, which went crazy with its newfound freedom, and I got it.

Freeze the handcuffs.

I gave her a soft nod, checking the surrounding cops to see if they had witnessed Maya or her quality mime-work. They still talked in small circles, glancing toward me to make sure I wasn't getting any ideas.

Unfortunately for them, I was, and Maya set them in motion. "*Te desiderari me*! You missed me, and you'll never catch me now!" she yelled from across the street.

A few cops turned her way, recognition flashing across their faces. Four took off after her, determined to make the dumb girl who had gotten away pay for coming back. That left two with me, who, although they remained close, watched the action across the street.

I went to work on my handcuffs, freezing my hands and wrists. I didn't know how cold I would need to be for the metal to freeze, so I mustered as much power as I could. I could feel the chill on my back as the sound of the freezing handcuffs grew. A male cop looked back toward me, but I sat like a log, pretending to have no interest in the events around me. He turned back to watch as Maya sprinted from the police, leading them down a separate street.

The cuffs cracked and broke around my wrist with a muffled *clack*. I bolted upright, darting past the two cops who realized where the sound had come from. I crossed the street, ignoring the horns that blasted all around me. Racing down the sidewalk,

I weaved between the tourists and citizens who filmed the action in front of them instead of helping the cops who screamed "Stop!" behind me.

Ducking into an alley, I reversed direction, turning back to face the street. Bringing both arms up, a wall of ice erupted from the cement, rising multiple stories into the air and blocking off any entrance into the alley. Immediately, a sharp pain hammered in my chest. I ignored it as I kept running, spitting out small chunks of ice that formed in my mouth. My breath was chilled, but it warmed quickly from the exertion.

The other side of the alley opened back up into another street, this one much less populated. I crossed it, scanning for any cops, but the street and sidewalks were empty.

I repeated this same process, taking turns down side streets and cutting through alleys, all the while trying to stay aware of where the stadium had been. I had no idea how I was going to meet up with Maya, or if I wanted to.

I'd successfully lost the cops, as well as myself, after fifteen minutes of this. I slowed to a walk, taking in new sights of the city. Every siren made my heart skip a beat, but none were directed at me, and I continued walking, looking for a map or a familiar building, doing my best to keep down the growing panic.

As the sun hung low over the city skyline, I was on a concrete path that snaked through well-trimmed grass, protected from the rest of the city by budding trees. The quiet park was much needed, and I breathed deep as the sweet blossoms flooded my senses. A few others enjoying the evening strolled by me, none taking interest in me as they passed by. I stopped again, filling my lungs with the sweet summer air when a hand gripped the top of my shoulder.

I whirled around, the ring buzzing, forming the hilt of a sword in my hand. The hand slid off my shoulder, grabbing my left wrist, preventing it from moving. Maya's soft brown eyes met mine, her tan skin glowing in the ambient park lighting, a look of calm confidence on her face, like sneaking up on people and grabbing them was something she did all the time. Though I was slightly taller, her attitude and poise were intimidating, daring me to try something.

"I've been following you for a while, but man, you're fast. It took me a while to catch up."

She was so... close. I struggled with words, finally getting them out. "You left me."

"Sorry about that. I came back."

"Why?" I asked.

"Because I didn't want you to get arrested and taken away?"

"Is that because of me, or because it's your job?"

"Can both be true?"

I didn't have an answer.

After seconds of silence, she asked, "Do you have a brain freeze or something?"

"I can still have those?"

She rolled her eyes, releasing my wrist and walking past me, bumping shoulders as she passed. "Come on, Maledictus. I think the hotel is this way."

I took a moment to process what had happened, then jogged to catch up with her.

"Look, I really am sorry for splitting up. I didn't think they'd all go after you," she said. "I can tell you don't trust people, and I understand why. But I came back, and I will do whatever I need to do to earn your trust."

"Why?"

"Because I need to, Jaden. And, although it may not seem like it, you'll want people like Vincent and me on your side back home. We can help you learn, train, that sort of stuff. Dare I say be your friends?" she asked with a playful jab on my arm.

"How'd you learn to do that?" I asked, changing the conversation.

"Do what?"

"Track me, fighting, really everything you've done since I've known you."

"Vincent taught me a lot of that, but I also learned from being a Searcher."

"You're also a Searcher?"

"Sure am," she said, a twinge of pride filling her voice. As if sensing what I was going to ask next, she kept going. "I wanted to do more than just work as a Medela all day. Kind of like you and school here on Earth. It's boring, right? You wanted a thrill, which is why you agreed to come with us. My mom wasn't happy when I left and went to train as a Searcher, but I had to. I owed it to somebody."

"Who?"

"My cousin, Sofia. We grew up together, inseparable. We had a pact that we would work as Searchers for your mother, Queen Iris, to do our best to make Arrortha a better place, and fight against Ian. When we got our powers, we got different ones. She was given Crescere, and they expected her to grow food and plants and stuff, but that didn't stop her. I hadn't planned on getting Medela, and I thought I would be more helpful working for my mom."

We turned a corner, the LED city streetlights flooding the scarcely populated sidewalk.

"Sofia kept her end of the pact, joining the Searchers right away. She got her first job a couple of years later. It was a simple one." She paused, taking a shaky breath. "We hadn't talked since she joined. She came to say goodbye before she left, but I purposely hung with Vincent that night so I wouldn't see her." She wiped a tear from her eye. "She never came back. I waited for months. Finally, I couldn't take it anymore. I had to know what happened. I joined the Searchers with the sole purpose of finding her, and I did.... Just not before Ian did."

"I'm sorry."

"Don't be. It was my fault. But I've sworn to myself every day that if I was ever given a job to protect someone, I wouldn't fail."

She paused, letting silence fill the air. "Do you remember on the train when you asked why I was trying to teach you not to be useless? Well, when Queen Iris was looking for people to go to Earth to rescue *the* Maledictus, I was the first volunteer. What better way to get revenge against Ian than rescue his enemy's son? I didn't think I'd get chosen, but your mom asked me personally to go. Vincent volunteered as soon as he heard. Queen Iris wanted someone with more experience, but no one was willing to try something so dangerous, and he was adamant. She appointed Lucinda to go with us."

A siren sounded in the distance, making us walk a little faster.

"We trained for days before we left. Fighting, healing, even phantoms."

"What's a phantom?"

"It's like a dream. A strong Desolate, or many working together, can create one then enter it into your mind. From there, everything is normal, but they can control what you see, what happens in it, everything like that. They're dangerous, so we use them rarely, but for this, we had to. We guessed what you would look like, how you would fight, what we would have to say to you, things like that."

I wondered if my "dream" hadn't been a dream at all.

"In every phantom you were tall, muscular, white-haired, and invincible. I started doubting myself; how was I going to help *you*? I'd never been so nervous as I was when we knocked on that front door. But when you opened it, you didn't look anything like that. And then Noah attacked you, and no offense, you weren't invincible, either. You were scared, and just so... lost. You were a normal kid. It's my job to protect you, but at the same time, I *want* to. I want you to make it back home to your mom. I want you to trust me. That's why I'm trying to teach you all these things. For you and me." She whispered, "I can't fail someone else again."

"I think you're doing fine so far. I *am* still alive."

"You can thank yourself for that. I'm just trying to keep up."

She stopped walking, turning to face the building in front of us. To my surprise, the crappy hotel we'd been placed in loomed over us. Most of the front windows were darkened. I wondered if we were the only occupants.

"Anyway, here we are. Should probably get back inside before anyone else tries to arrest you," she said.

Nobody else tried to arrest me as we made our way into the lobby and up the stairs to our room. Maya knocked once on the door and waited for it to be answered. A worried-looking Vincent flung it open, relieved to see one of us standing there.

"I was beginning to get worried. Are you okay?" he asked.

Maya nodded.

"Anything happen?"

"Nope," Maya said, pushing past him and into the room, with me following behind. Vincent looked, no, glared at her and beyond, shaking his head at the far side of the room, where Lucinda faced away from me, talking to the wall. I went deeper into the room, eyeing her, thinking maybe she had totally lost it. She shifted her shoulders, and when she did, I could see what she was talking to.

The air swirled around her, looking like ripples in water on a windy day. The ripples surrounded a crystal-clear image displayed in a weird video hologram, a single woman filling it, a grim but determined look on her face. I recognized her as the woman from my dream. Dark brown hair, sparkling eyes that softened when she saw me standing behind Lucinda. A wistful smile crossed her face when she looked at me. Something else flashed on her face, and I recognized a look of hope.

"He's so grown up," the woman said, tears brimming the corners of her eyes.

"Much bigger than when I brought him," Lucinda said, turning to look at me now, too.

I was captivated by the woman, unable to form a single word. Eventually, I got one out. "Mom?"

"*Dulcis puer meus.* My heart has waited for this moment for the last fifteen years. Please, hurry, and get back to me."

I nodded, and she turned back to Lucinda. "Take care of him, and make sure all of you get back in one piece."

Lucinda said, "Yes, ma'am," before pressing something on her necklace, the video disappearing.

"Listen, people," she said, addressing everyone in the room, including Ollie, whose hair was still wet as he exited the bathroom. "Ian is sending more Venators to the portal, meaning we've got to get there before they do. So congratulations, Jaden, we will be flying after all. Everyone grab your stuff. We're leaving right now."

We had nothing to grab, the girls claimed what they'd put in the second room, and we left the hotel room shortly after. I flipped the room's keycards onto the front desk as we passed by, earning a scowl from the same desk worker. Five minutes later, we piled into the back of a taxi, heading for O'Hare International Airport and a flight out of the city.

Chapter Eleven

An hour later, and with added tension, we arrived at the airport. Lucinda ushered everyone out of the taxi, guiding us through the evening breeze and into the building. We hunted the flight trackers that sat behind the check-in counters, looking for the next flight to Denver, regardless of the airline. I spotted one, pulling Lucinda and the wad of cash to the counter, where we were greeted by a tired-looking man with a thick fireman's mustache. He raised his eyebrows when we asked him about that night's late evening flight to Denver, but after typing on his computer for a while, he saw the plane was only half-full.

"How much are the tickets?" I asked, grabbing the rest of the cash from Lucinda.

"Eight hundred sixty-eight total, if you don't have bags. I need IDs first."

Lucinda handed him the three fake Earth passports, while I

gave him mine and Ollie's social security cards. He eyed them closely. I tried my best to look calm as he looked at each passport, then up at the person whose it claimed to be. After what felt like ages, he sighed and took the money for the tickets.

"The flight will be out of gate B10. It's straight that way," he said, pointing to a large, cavernous hallway behind us. "You'll go right past it. Can't miss it."

I took the tickets, thanking him.

The passports got us through security, despite Lucinda demanding to know why she had to remove her shoes to walk through the scanner. At first, she refused to leave her staff, only agreeing to do so once security threatened to have her arrested. I used the distraction to toss Maya the dagger around my ankle once she made it through the metal detector. She hid it from view while she put her shoes back on.

I got the knife back from her as we sat in the gate waiting area. With just under an hour until the plane was scheduled to leave, I surveyed the rest of the passengers, my unease growing as I scanned each one. Almost thirty in total, and each one eyed me, even as I checked on others waiting. After five minutes of this, I leaned over to Maya. "What are the chances these people are all Desolates?"

"Almost *nulla*. Why?" she asked, scrunching her face. I told her about the staring problem. As she gauged each one, concern grew on her face. "Okay, maybe not zero. It has to be Esham."

We looked around, not trying to be subtle in finding him. But we found nothing, and returned to facing the window and the illuminated runways outside.

"How has he been able to follow us the whole time?" I asked.

"He knows where we're going," Vincent answered, having heard the question.

"Yeah, Denver. Why not wait for us there, then? We've gone to Pittsburgh, Cleveland, Indianapolis, now Chicago, and yet he or somebody else has been waiting for us in each city. Even in D.C., they knew to find us at the train station."

"You're cursed, and he's one of the most powerful Desolates in Arrortha. Maybe he can sense that, and knows where you are at all times," Maya suggested.

I wasn't buying it. "Wouldn't it make sense for him to tell me that? Tell me he will always be following?"

Vincent scoffed at the suggestion. "Nobody knows why Esham does what he does. He likes to play mind games; to get you thinking exactly like he is now."

"How do you know this?"

"I asked Lucinda. I like to know who I'm up against, and she worked with him for a long time. I'm sure she'd be willing to tell you all the tricks he would pull."

It was odd, but I let it go.

"Where in Denver is this portal?" I asked Maya.

"Under the airport."

"We should've just flown," I said, shaking my head.

"Based on everything that has happened, I agree. But I'm guessing you wouldn't have agreed to go, and you certainly wouldn't have had so much fun."

I rolled my eyes but laughed. "I still don't fully believe you it exists."

"Really? I can understand your babysitter trying to kill you not being enough. That could happen to anyone. But giant snakes that hiss your name? A guy who can talk to you in your mind? You being able to create ice at will? That's not enough for you? You really do have trust issues."

"Yeah, I guess I do."

"You'll see," was all she said in reply.

* * *

The call to board came half an hour later. Our seats were near the front, meaning we were some of the first passengers on the plane. I sat, anxious, as each rider passed, but no one made eye contact as they moved their way to the back, their effect from earlier seemingly gone.

My fears came to fruition as the last group began boarding. Esham strolled onto the plane, looking like he didn't have a single care in the world, going as far as to give me a cheeky smile and a sarcastic finger wave.

His voice materialized in my head. *Almost there, Maledictus! I trust you've started to realize your greater purpose.*

I did my best to ignore it, instead watching Ollie fiddle with his seatbelt until the plane began to taxi for the runway.

As we climbed, the cabin lights dimmed. The captain sounded over the intercom, announcing our flight would arrive in Denver in about three hours. As the PA system crackled and turned off, a new voice sounded in my head.

Nowhere to run now, Maledictus, although you seem more like a fighter, just like your dad was. Like Ian is. You two could rule Arrortha forever. But that's for a later date. Now, I just want to talk. You're a kid with a great deal of responsibility, and all I want to do is help. I know I've been painted as the bad guy, but a story needs one of those, and everyone is the hero in their own story, no?

Tell me, Maledictus, are you the hero in your own story? Who is the villain? Is it Ian? Me? Maybe even one of those two sitting next to you?

I looked to my sides, where Vincent and Maya sat flanking me.

Can you sense it, Jaden? How else would I know where you're going to be before you do? You of all kids should know that not everyone is as they seem. But me, Maledictus? I've been straight with you, and so has Ian. Your decision must be made soon. It would be a shame for you to be, how do you Earth dwellers say it, dead on arrival?

Then it was silent. My conscious mind was the only thing wreaking havoc in my head, but it didn't need the help. Esham had told me either Maya or Vincent was working for him, but was he lying? *Can you sense it?* How else would he know about that conversation? I suddenly felt trapped, unable to decide who, if anyone, I could trust.

His words consumed me for almost an hour and a half. Thankfully, neither Vincent nor Maya tried to talk to me, because I don't know what I would've said. I thought about my situation, like a trapped rat going through a maze, where every corner unveiled a new horror. And yet, the only way I could go was forward. It had been made clear that going back to my previous life wasn't an option, and one I didn't want to choose if it was. The prospect of my real mother being alive and waiting for me to return was enough. But what if Esham wasn't playing mind games? What if I had a choice? I knew nothing about Arrortha. What if my mother turned out to be the villain?

No. He's trying to make me think that. She's my mom. I was going to get back to her despite whatever stood in my way.

What did I know about the Desolate power? Esham was able to get into my head, I could only assume by sheer will and force. If he could do it to me, surely Maledictus could do it back. I closed my eyes, bringing my thoughts to him. His face appeared in my mind, and I took a shot.

Esham.

His name hung in my mind, running into a barrier that stopped it from getting out. I tried again. *Esham.* Again, the name hung in the air. Maybe it wasn't so simple. I focused on his face, putting as much force behind the thought as I could, like a kid making a wish as they blew out their birthday candles. *Esham!* This time, the name seemed to push through, and like a breeze, it floated away. I soon got a reply.

Yes, Maledictus?

A chill went down my spine as my subconscious merged with his. I felt lost, like a child walking through a dark forest, glowing eyes melting in and out of shadows, ducking behind trees, but always watching. I was in his mind, and it was a grim, calamitous place. Steeling myself, I prepared for the conversation ahead.

I'm not joining Ian.

You'd be wise to wait on that decision until you see what awaits you on the ground.

It doesn't matter, I'll get through it, I thought to him, mustering as much courage as I could. My subconscious battled his, fighting through the tar pit that was Esham's mind.

You've gotten much bolder. Stupider, but bolder. I admire that, and it'll be useful, but your anger is misplaced.

I've learned a little about who I am. I don't have to lie down anymore. I can stand up to people like you.

Stultus puer. All I have done is show you who you are, and this is the conclusion you have come to?

All you've done is try to kill me and my brother.

Kill? Oh, no. Those serpents were no match for Maledictus. As for your brother, how else would you learn how capable you truly are?

Maya had to keep me alive!

Hardly. You fought through that on your own while you walked through that field. Tell me, Jaden, what is it you truly desire in this life?

I didn't answer, my thoughts drawn back to what I'd seen in the field.

I think I know, Jaden. You want one person, one single person, who cares about you and won't betray you. You've convinced yourself there is no such person, yet you push forward, looking for light in your land of eternal darkness.

And that person is you? You want me to choose you over my mom?

She was the first to abandon you, Jaden.

Because of Ian! Who also killed my dad.

Your dad died an unnecessary death. One you can thank that old hag sitting by you for. Everything bad in your life has come from someone claiming they're trying to help you.

Like you're doing right now?

It was muted for a moment as Esham's mind darkened still.

Despite your incorrect assumptions, my offer still stands, Maledictus. You've met your mother, and I understand your reasoning, but it is wrong. When you see how your potential is wasted and change your mind in Arrortha, you know how to reach me. If you make it that far.

I was kicked out of his mind, my subconscious sent scrambling back to my head. I was frustrated by the mind games, although well aware this was his intention. Still, I was nervous about what awaited me on the ground. As if on cue, the seatbelt sign flashed as the pilot's voice came over the PA system, announcing we had begun our final descent. I took a deep, measured breath as the plane's nose tilted forward. I'd come so far since leaving the Edwards' house, but something told me the toughest challenge was yet to come.

I fully expected Esham to attack before the plane landed, but nothing came, and shortly after, the wheels of the plane touched down and we began our slow taxi to the terminal. The sky was completely dark, now nearing midnight. Bright lights flashed everywhere, illuminating runways and work vehicles alike.

The plane stopped next to its jet bridge, a hiss sounding in the cabin as the brakes locked. I looked around for snakes before realizing where the sound had come from. People began standing, grabbing their luggage from the overhead bins and clogging the aisles. Maya and Vincent stood in front of and back of me. I hated being between them, especially now that I feared one, or both, was working with the psychotic Desolate at the back of the plane.

Multiple gasps, followed by, "What are those things?" sounded from near the back of the cabin.

We looked back, where people pointed out the plane

windows, others crowding close to see. I looked out my own window, horrified by what I saw: A pair of panthers, which is the best way I can describe them, darted across the runways, making a beeline for the plane. I squinted, trying to better understand what I was looking at as they closed the distance.

They were very large cats, that much was clear. That was where the normalcy ended. Their skin reflected light, gleaming in different directions as the duo took long, graceful strides. As they neared, I realized their skin wasn't skin at all, but metal, aligned in the shape of a panther's skeleton. Slender, metallic tails extended from the rear of the cat, flicking in different directions as they weaved between other planes and vehicles. As they got to within one hundred feet, I realized I could see right through them, like they really were just hollow iron skeletons.

Esham's voice entered my mind. *Your mother is a false hope. Join me now and my pets will not harm you or your brother. If you don't, I can—*

I kicked him out, focusing on clearing my head. His voice stopped, and I was the only occupant.

Outside, one of the iron cats leapt off the ground, landing on top of the plane, sending a loud bang throughout the cabin. People screamed as the sound of metal claws dug into the roof, racing toward the front.

We were the first to react, forcing our way into the aisle and toward the front of the plane. Both the airplane and cockpit door opened as we reached it.

The largest cat appeared outside the cockpit window, snarling at us; glass cracked and splintered as its claws drove into it, getting stuck. The pilots ducked for cover, then fled past us, deeper into the plane.

We ran off the plane as the cat tried to enter.

We rounded a corner on the bridge just as a group of men blocked the far end, their swords out and ready.

"Ian's Venators," Maya said. "They've been waiting for us."

Metal clashed with metal above us as the panther gave up on the airplane, jumped onto the bridge and sprinted toward the airport terminal.

Vincent took charge, stepping in front of me, Windweaver already up and pointing at the Venators opposite us. Their eyes went wide as a blast of air erupted from the ax, sending swords and men slamming against the walls, ceiling, and even back into the terminal.

We entered the waiting area as Ian's people started to gather themselves, but sprinted past them, continuing past other air travelers, who watched in bewilderment at the scene unfolding. Vincent continued leading the way, weaving through traffic and down long airport hallways. Nobody attempted to stop us, and I'd yet to hear the metal clicking of iron claws on the tile floors.

That soon came to a screeching halt, literally, as the sound echoed around the airport. We were met with several more of Ian's Venators, as they lined up to block the escalators that would take us down to the lower floors. Both sides stopped, surveying each other.

Lucinda stood next to me, Ollie right behind her, a terrified mask on his face.

"Jaden, tell the ring 'Adustum,'" she said. I must've looked confused, because she told me to "Do it" immediately after.

The ring buzzed on my finger, and I commanded it using the same word Lucinda had. The ring flashed, and my fingers curled around the grip of a single long sword. The weapon was a brilliant white, almost blinding in the airport lights.

"That," Lucinda said, "is Adustum. *Frostbite.* The true Glacies sword; your father's."

I felt the blade, which was as polished and sharp as anything I'd seen. The sword seemed to feed off me, amping up for the fight ahead. I stepped beside Vincent, who looked at the sword, then back to the Venators with a *Let's do this* grin.

Vincent and I led the way, despite us being outnumbered two to four. I met with two on the right, while Vincent veered left to take the other two. The first hunter stepped forward to meet me, swinging his sword in an aggressive slash. I deflected it, rotating my body to face the other hunter, ready for his attack. He was a younger guy, no more than five years older than me, but he hesitated, waiting back instead of attacking. I wondered if he had been forced into this like I had, and I felt bad for him for a moment.

That moment quickly passed. My left side was exposed to the other fighter, a man well older than either of us, who sneered a gap-toothed smile, thinking he had already beaten me. I brought both hands over my head, my sword hanging down next to me, catching his flush as he swung again. I used the movement to pivot, Frostbite whipping around until it sliced into the back of the man's leg. He howled in pain as the wound grew red and froze over.

Frostbite. The true Glacies sword, I thought.

The other kid seemed to gain a bit of courage from his teammate being hurt—he charged wildly, slashing his sword at least twice before he was within a distance he could harm me. Again, I almost felt bad for him, but the past few days I'd discovered a new part of me, and with that, a sort of code for the future: Don't try to kill me first, and I won't go all *Maledictus* on you.

The kid swung a third time, this time well within range. I sidestepped his blind attack, countering with a backhand of my own. His sword arced backward, stopping mine in a surprise defense. I was momentarily stunned, but the Glacies in me spiked, and I dropped into a roll as the older Venator's blade slammed down behind me, where I'd been moments ago.

The screech of one of the metal skeleton cats alarmed me, telling me I'd have to hurry up and end this fight. I went on the offensive, running toward the younger guy. When I was just feet away, I raised my right hand, and a block of ice rose from the tile floor. I used it as a trampoline, leaping into the air as the hunter lunged his sword low and fast, trying to take out my ankles. His face screamed surprise as I landed on him, driving the hilt of Frostbite into his forehead. He crumpled to the ground, unconscious and out of the fight.

The older man with the missing teeth was none too happy, bellowing as he swung with all his might. Frostbite caught and absorbed the energy of the attack, freezing the two weapons together. We locked eyes, his glaring with pure hatred. Suddenly, tears formed in the corners of his and he cried out, releasing his sword as he too fell to the ground. I was baffled, but Maya had buried her spear deep in the side of his thigh. He screamed again as she removed it.

The screech from a skelecat drowned out the other cries.

Maya grabbed my wrist.

"We have to go. Now," Vincent said, appearing at our side. "We're going down. The tunnels are that way." He pointed down the escalator, where they opened into a spacious ground-floor courtyard that disappeared underneath the floor we were on. I shook free of Maya's grasp, still unconvinced she wasn't going to use it to stab me with the spear herself and searched for Ollie. He and Lucinda were already on the escalators, using the stairs as fast as his little legs would let him. Another skelecat cried out, and we followed behind, taking the stairs two at a time.

We fled through the ground level, our weapons drawing the attention of everyone we passed. Panicked shrieks erupted behind us, followed by the sound of metal on metal and the clinking of iron claws on the floor. I turned to see both skelecats racing toward us as other passengers scurried out of their way.

Vincent, Maya, and I caught up to Lucinda and Ollie. We all turned, facing the cats, who growled angrily thirty feet away.

"Take him. Keep going to the tunnels. We will meet you on the other side," Vincent said, talking to Lucinda but motioning to Ollie.

"Get him back in one piece," she said, pointing to me. "Portal to Highmoore. We will have the whole city ready for anyone who tries to follow."

She gave us one last "good luck" as she ushered Ollie away and down the hall. I hadn't taken my eyes off the skelecats, but now I gave them my full attention, pushing away the thought that I may have just seen Ollie for the last time.

I took a deep breath, readying myself. With Frostbite in my left hand, I remembered Lucinda's lessons with my right, using it to create a shield of solid ice. I gripped it tight, peering over the top at the skelecats, who now moved in, preparing for the fight.

The cat nearest me kept its eyes, which were small and glowing orange dots in the middle of the hollowed eye sockets, trained on me, while the other one moved in a wide arc, getting on Vincent's side.

The cat lunged as he swung his ax, the blade and metal shoulder meeting with a *clunk.* The two separated, a noise coming from the panther, who, with only a minimal dent in its shoulder, looked hardly affected by the exchange.

I dodged to the left, narrowly avoiding the giant paw of the skelecat in front of me. I brought Frostbite up, the tip just feet away from the cat, which hissed, looking for a way around the sword.

It feigned an attack from the left, leaping far to its right, where it swiped another powerful paw at me. I countered with Frostbite, flailing the weapon and connecting it with the paw. The impact knocked me backward, where I steadied myself with the shield. I recovered as quickly as I could, expecting the cat to be on top of me any second. But as I whipped around, the cat stayed back, trying to shake itself free from the ice that had formed where it and Frostbite had collided.

Another crack of an ax on a metal cat sounded beside me, this one leading to a much louder, and pained, snarl from the cat. I didn't have time to check before my cat was attacking again. I blocked one, then a second, then a third swipe with the shield, each time the metal claws digging a little deeper into the frozen face of it. On the fourth try, the cat leapt up into the air and down. I did what I could to block it, but the iron spears it used for claws dug deep into the ice. I was forced to let go of the shield to avoid having my wrist broken. The skelecat shook its paw, sending the shield spinning like a frisbee.

The panther lunged before I could make another one. I dove out of the way, but not fast enough. Four of the cat's five claws caught my right thigh, leaving gashes across it. I winced in pain as I took my hand to the wound. It returned bloodied. The skelecat circled me, the predator instinct inside of it looking for the final weakness in its prey. I stood, the pain from the wounds surprisingly dull. I knew as soon as adrenaline wore off it was going to hurt, but right now it was somewhere around number ten on my list of most pressing issues.

I stabbed with Adustum, hoping the surprise attack might shift the balance of the fight. The attack worked as the blade connected with the tip of the cat's nose. Unfortunately, all I succeeded in doing was making the cat's face very cold. It pawed at its nose, retreating slightly to clear the ice. I used the distraction to check on Vincent.

He had Maya helping him, though she wasn't doing much more than being a good distraction. But I'll admit, she did her job well. She'd run back and forth, sometimes poking the cat with her spear, sometimes slamming down on its back with the shaft. One time she grabbed the cat's tail, barely avoiding the claws she got as a response. Vincent timed the lack of attention perfectly. He stabbed the ax forward and twisted, getting it stuck between ribs in the cat's body. He yelled at Maya to duck, then pushed Windweaver forward, and a blast of air spurted from the ax. The air swirled in the skelecat, blasting metal ribs and hindquarters outward. Many were impaled in a wheeled luggage cart that had been left by a frightened passenger, the force pushing it across the hallway and toward me.

Vincent untwisted the ax, removing it from the skelecat, which now teetered awkwardly as it tried to compensate for its missing half. Following one final swift kick, the cat toppled over and lay still.

I was awestruck, only saved from my flying panther at the last second, as my Glacies power screamed at me. Ten five-inch iron claws grazed my hair as I fell to the floor, the cat tumbling and rolling past me. We both jumped to our feet. I sprinted away, the panther in hot pursuit.

The luggage cart had drifted all the way across the hallway, resting a few feet away from the wall. A hasty plan danced in my mind. The cat was only feet behind me as I planted one foot on a black hard-shell suitcase, leaping high and... straight into the wall. I held Frostbite in my left as my right hand and foot contacted the wall, freezing to it. I hung like Spiderman as the cat crashed into the luggage cart below, twisting frantically to free itself of the fallen luggage and find me. It searched, spinning circles, utterly confused as to how I'd completely disappeared.

It settled on Vincent and Maya, who stared dumbfounded at me. The cat looked up as I dropped from the wall. Frostbite pointed down and at the center point of its body, directly between its shoulders. I transferred as much Glacies power as I could to the sword, which was glowing hot white as I fell.

The energy-filled Frostbite entered the skelecat's body, freezing everything it touched. I did all I could to bring the blade into contact with as much metal as possible, running it side to side and front to back. Finally, I leapt back, bringing the sword out in front of me, ready for more attacks, but there were none coming. The cat's joints were white with frost, frozen stiff. They trembled, giving away from the weight of the material. Metal crashed, and where the skelecat had once been was now a pile of scrap iron.

It was calm as the metal came to a rest, but as I caught my breath, a new sound registered in my ears: cheering. I looked up to a swarm of phones facing my direction. Several daring passengers had made their way back down the hall. Some looked in shock, some in amazement, and a few with wide smiles, knowing they had just captured the Internet's next viral video.

I gave a sheepish nod, aware I was going to be on every television and phone screen soon. I caught my reflection in a window as I made my way back to Vincent and Maya. What had once been the whites of my eyes glowed completely light blue now, leaving hues on my eyelids and cheeks.

They both noticed the new phenomenon.

"We're close," Vincent said, looking more nervous. "He's getting stronger."

Maya stood next to him, confounded by the color. She looked in awe as she said, "They're even prettier than in the phantom."

Commotion brought our attention to the onlookers, where more Venators with swords pushed through the crowd, who cleared a path, but kept recording as their night continued to get weirder.

Vincent led us in the other direction. We sprinted through hallway after hallway, Ian's Venators chasing and yelling at us. After what felt like we had run through the entire airport, Vincent kicked open a door with a large red "Maintenance" sign overhead. The door led to another passage, which soon led down a set of stairs. We took them two at a time, reaching the bottom and continuing on. After a couple of turns, we arrived in a darkened hallway, illuminated by a single viburnum, which swirled brightly, making it look like blue flames climbed the walls.

The hallway was quiet behind us, but even so, we rushed, stopping next to the glowing ball. Across from us, a large hole in the wall opened menacingly, a faint glow coming from deep within. Vincent and Maya stepped through, climbing over large concrete chunks that had once made up the wall. I took a deep breath, my heart pounding, my leg beginning to throb from the cuts made by the skelecat's claws.

The pair in front of me waited, looking back and beckoning me to pass them. I hated being in front of the two that were possibly working for Ian, but I saw no other choice. I gripped Frostbite a little tighter and stepped into the tunnel.

Chapter Twelve

The inside of the tunnel was dim and damp. Moisture pooled from the humidity before dripping down the rock walls. Viburnums placed every fifty feet lit up small portions of the tunnel, providing a sort of breadcrumb path for us to follow. Our shadows danced on the tunnel walls, their shapes morphed and distorted by the swirling glow of the ice balls. There was nothing beyond the sound of our footfalls. No sounds of feet smacking the floor from those behind us, no growling of some new creature trying to kill me, not even a hum from the airport overhead.

"Are they still chasing us?" I asked, if for nothing more than to hear any sort of sound. Neither one answered me for a bit, driving up my suspicion. I glanced back as I walked, still following the lights on the wall.

"They don't want to be trapped down here with you," Vincent finally said. "Or they have more people waiting at the portal. Who knows?"

We walked on in silence for another five minutes, the viburnum guiding us down paths that turned right and left, even taking us down a set of stairs. Maya had caught up to me, now walking by my side, as Vincent stayed behind, checking over his shoulder.

"What did Lucinda mean by taking the portal to Highmoore? Don't portals open to one spot on the other side?" I asked her, though now my voice felt loud in the slim corridors.

"It's complicated," was all she said at first. Ten seconds later, she kept going. "There's only one entrance on either side. But you can exit the portal anywhere, if you have a name for the place. But nothing too specific. Does that make sense?"

I shook my head. She continued. "This portal can't land you straight at your mother's side in the castle, but it can jump you to the center of Highmoore. You can choose any kingdom in Arrortha, but each time you'll end up in the middle of that kingdom."

"How does th—"

She cut me off. "Don't ask me how it works, because I have no idea. Nobody does, unless their name is Krera, and even then, she may not know."

"But there is only one entrance on the Arrortha side?"

She nodded, facing forward, her eyes widening. I followed with mine. The line of snowballs ended as the tunnel turned left. Instead, thin, faint strips of light beamed from around the corner. They too flickered and danced on the rocky floor.

My heart, if it was possible, beat even harder.

We rounded the corner. The portal loomed in front of me, stretching from the floor to the ceiling in an oblong rectangle shape. It filled most of the tunnel, leaving only a few small gaps between the corners and the rocky wall. A white ring ran around the inside of the portal, morphing into gray contrast before turning solid black near the middle. Like the rest of the tunnel, the portal was bathed in silence, leaving nothing but our breathing as the only sound.

I was feet away from the portal, amazed at its presence, only now fully believing what I'd been told for the past days.

Maya walked up beside me, smiling at me.

I think I surprised her by smiling back. "You were telling the truth."

"Yes, Jaden. You really are who we say you are."

"That means my mom is alive?"

"And waiting for you on the other side of this portal."

Esham's words still nagged at me, demanding an answer before I could enter Arrortha. Turning to face her, I drew in a breath, gripping Frostbite a little tighter.

"What about Esham?"

"What about him?" she asked, her eyebrows furrowing.

"He knew about our conversation. He told me that not everyone was as they seemed. That somebody trying to get me back was working with him and Ian."

"He's lying to you. None of us would work w—"

"That'd be me," Vincent interrupted her.

I turned to look at him, and for the second time in the brief four days we'd known each other, the blade of his knife was up against my throat.

"Oh, come on, don't act surprised. I've been telling him your every move from the moment we met; I wasn't exactly trying to hide it. Now," he adjusted the knife, the sharp edge pressing into my skin, threatening to cut it, "I don't want to kill the son of the queen, but if he were to try something stupid… I won't lose sleep."

"So, he can do his mind trick with you? How'd you do that without anyone noticing?" I asked, feeling the blade press a little harder with each movement.

"Actually, you made that part easy. You kept eyeing me when you thought I was looking out the hotel window in Chicago, but he was talking to me in my head, planning our next move. Honestly, I figured you suspected something. I'm just glad you're too timid to trust yourself."

I wanted to feel betrayed, but when I thought about it, I'd never really trusted him. Him holding the knife to my throat seemed pretty consistent with the rest of my life.

"What do you want?" I asked, glancing at Maya the best I could without moving my head. She remained still, either in shock or alliance.

"I *wanted* a lot of things to have worked out differently, so this part would be easier." He gave me a look that said *What can ya do?* before continuing. "Anyway, you're well aware of Esham's offer, but just in case you aren't as smart as I give you credit for, here it is: You come with me, work with Ian, and you two rule Arrortha. Everyone is happy. Everyone but Esham, I guess. You really made him mad. He just wants you dead." He shrugged.

"What do you get out of this?"

"I get an army and the freedom to use it how it's meant to be used: to hunt. At least Lucinda was a Glacies, she understood our place. Your mother ruined Highmoore. People used to fear the kingdom, respect us. Now they just walk all over us. Ian's had enough of it. So have I, and so have many others. It's time we strong ones stopped being held down by those less capable. Your mom would rather everyone be equally weak, and it's what will ruin Arrortha entirely. You're one of the strongest of them all, Jaden. Don't let yourself be dragged down. Now, give me the ring." His voice softened, but he kept the knife where it was. He pointed at Maya with the other hand, which still held his ax. "There's a place for you, too," he said to her. "Please, Maya, you're so much better than you think you are. I need someone as smart as you by my side, helping me."

She looked… hurt, and mad, and unless she was putting on a brilliant performance, was truly blindsided. She drew in a shaky breath before uttering a single word. "Why?"

"His offer was too good to pass up. It is for you, too. Both of you," he said now, turning his attention back to me. Frostbite still hung by my side, but he gave me no chance to use it.

"What if I say no?" I asked him.

Vincent pushed the blade even tighter as a response. "I have a knife against your windpipe, bro."

He adjusted his grip on his ax. "What's it going to be, Maledictus?"

In my peripheral vision, I could see Maya turn to face me too, as if what she would decide was based on my decision. I was silent for a moment, though I realized I'd made up my mind a couple of days ago. My father loved me enough to die for me. My mother, though in an entirely different world, was only steps away through the glowing portal. My only concern was his knife, but I was hoping Maya would help me with that.

"I'm going to choose the one who didn't curse me and kill my dad."

As I said it, I froze my hand, ready to try to get it between the knife and my skin, figuring a cut there would be better than one on my neck.

"Ian is giving you a chance to have more power than your dad could've ever hoped to give you. You didn't even know him."

"And that makes it better? I have the chance to meet at least *one* of my parents."

Vincent nodded slightly, digesting my answer. Then, to my surprise, removed the blade.

"That's too bad," he said. In one casual motion, he re-sheathed the knife, bringing the free hand to Windweaver's handle. With a new fire in his eyes, he swung the ax directly at my head.

Maya cried out, but I was way ahead of her, diving to the floor as sparks showered me from where the axe connected with the wall. Vincent tried to kick, but I brought my hands up, absorbing most of his shoe, as he barely caught the side of my cheek.

I flew to my feet, Frostbite in front of me. Vincent stared daggers at me from across the tunnel while Maya brought her spear out, heightening my senses. I still wasn't convinced I wasn't about to get a spear in the side, or worse.

But she turned the spear against Vincent, who looked both frustrated and saddened. His expression changed quickly though, hardening. He repositioned himself, sidestepping away from the portal. I mirrored him, ending up shoulder to shoulder with Maya.

Vincent attacked first, swinging Windweaver at me. Maya ducked out of the way, giving me more space. I deflected the attack with Adustum, the two blades meeting. Frozen shards of ice rained over my head and neck, melting and running down the sides of my face.

I countered the deflection with a slash of my own, Frostbite almost scraping the top of the tunnel. Vincent blocked the swing by grabbing the blade and handle of Windweaver, using the belly of the handle as a bar to catch Adustum. I expected the sword to slice through, but the two weapons met and stuck, leaving Vincent and me locked in a battle of strength.

He won that fight. The muscles in his arm bulged and flexed as he shoved forward, releasing the two weapons and staggering me backward. He followed the shove by pivoting on his feet, firing Windweaver's blade through the gap separating us. I kept stumbling, avoiding the ax. He readied again, this time backhanded. My Glacies and I were prepared, timing the swing and avoiding the blade that whistled by my stomach. I rushed forward, springing into the air. Vincent turned his body as my foot arced out, jump-kicking him in the ribs.

He gasped for air as I landed on my right knee, slamming it on the ground. We both stood, breathing hard, ten feet away from each other.

"Any chance you'd just hand the ring over?" Vincent asked, still panting. I stared back, trying to be as menacing as possible. He looked at the ground as he kept talking. "I was afraid of that. You know, Jaden, I really wish you would've said yes. You're just like Ian, and I like your style. Nobody could beat us."

I was about to tell him to shut up when Maya sprinted by me, her spear out, pointed straight at Vincent. He heard her approaching, shooting upright, blocking the spear with his ax. She swung again, wildly this time. It was predictable, and

Vincent dodged the attack before shouldering her to the ground. He raised the ax overhead, ready to strike it down on top of her, but hesitated.

I raced forward, covering the distance between him and me in a split second. He saw me out of the corner of his eye, but wasn't quick enough to react. Frostbite sliced deep into his lower leg, allowing Maya to scramble away as Vincent grabbed at the wound. He glared at me, gripping Windweaver tight, looking like a bull about to charge. Slowly, he hobbled at me, gritting his teeth with each step.

We traded a few attacks and blocks. I cut him a few times, but he was strong enough to avoid serious damage from Frostbite's sharp edges. I brought myself back to Hugo's basement, and the one training session I'd had with him. My Glacies went on autopilot, blocking each of his attacks while my mind traveled back to Indianapolis and the PVC pipes. I dissected every part of his motions, looking for weaknesses. I studied his attacks, how he would recover, even his footwork. All the while, my powers controlled my body, keeping me alive in the present.

I found what I was looking for, bringing my mind back just as my arms shot out to block a desperate attack from Vincent, who was tiring, the gash on his leg taking a toll as it froze over. I had a plan.

Adustum shone as I transferred more Glacies to it. Vincent noticed it, his eyes leaving mine to glance toward the sword. He looked nervous, the confidence he had before the fight started wavering.

I swung Frostbite with the same slash I'd done earlier in the fight. Just like before, he brought Windweaver up, preparing to block the attack the same way. This time I stopped the swing as it neared his weapon. My arm shot across my body, bypassing his block attempt, stabbing Frostbite backhanded, putting as much effort as I could muster into the attack. Vincent tried to adjust his deflection attempt, but it was too late. The Glacies sword dug deep into his side, gashing its way through his entire left flank.

Windweaver dropped to his side as he grabbed at the wound, doubled over in pain. Sweat beads formed and ran down his face as the wound bled onto the ground below. His labored breathing echoed in the tunnel, the sound covering my panting. Maya was back on her feet, pointing her spear in his direction, a rabid look on her face. We split as we stepped cautiously toward Vincent, who had dropped to a knee, head hanging.

He mumbled something I didn't understand; I presume in Latin. I looked at Maya, hoping to get a translation, but she spoke back in the same language. His head lifted, turning to face her. His voice softened as he spoke. "*Me paenitet.*"

I sensed motion and brought Frostbite up as I faced Vincent. He had turned Windweaver toward me, the head of the ax staring me down. Air blasted from it, lifting me off my feet and sending me deeper into the tunnel. I landed hard, losing my grip on Adustum as the sword went airborne.

My whole body hurt, old and new wounds working together to make every move difficult. My head pounded, but the Glacies power in me demanded I get up and continue the fight. I climbed to my knees first, before standing on shaky legs. Frostbite had skidded on the ground, now resting against the far wall. I held my hand out, commanding the ring to bring the sword to me. The ring obliged as Frostbite flew through the air, the grip landing in my palm. With the weapon back in my grasp, and now fully annoyed, I turned my attention back to the traitor.

The situation was much worse now than before I'd felt Windweaver's wrath. Vincent was back on his feet, the knife back in his hand. This time, though, it was pressed against Maya's throat, who was trapped by his powerful arms.

"You always were a fighter. Heal me," he said, his voice harsh, but noticeably weaker. She refused, only to have the blade dug deeper into her skin. She winced, reaching her hand down to his wound.

"All of it."

Their faces changed: Vincent's to relief, Maya's to pure agony. After a refreshed sigh, he looked at me, though he quickly looked away, looking at my feet.

"We're going to walk by you, Maledictus. Don't be a hero. For her sake, I suggest you and that sword don't move. And unless you want to take an ice sculpture home, I suggest you don't make eye contact with her either."

He shuffled, dragging Maya along with him, who did nothing to help. Tears streamed down her face from the pain, but she was silent. I stayed where I was as they moved past me. With the portal behind him, Vincent spoke again, this time much more confidently.

"Good choice. Now, how about that ring?"

"Why?"

"Ian has his reasons. You're running out of time, Jaden. What are you going to save? The ring or the girl?"

"The… ring," Maya croaked, leading to Vincent squeezing tighter.

Four days into my new life, and I already faced a choice that had no appropriate answer. Lucinda had told me how powerful this ring was, and I'd experienced the abilities it gave its wearer. In the wrong hands…. And yet, this smart, troubled, and annoyingly persistent girl was the closest thing I'd had to a friend, ever, even if I didn't trust her yet.

I slipped the ring off my finger. Frostbite disappeared instantly, gone too was the glow produced by the sword, leaving the portal as the only light source in the hallway.

"Put it on the ground and back away."

I did as I was told, though I grabbed Noah's dagger I'd kept around my ankle, as it was now my only weapon if Vincent attacked again. He didn't. Instead, he threw Maya toward me, who crumpled to the ground as I caught her. Vincent grabbed the ring, slipping it onto his finger before stepping up to the portal.

"I'll see you around, Maledictus," he said. He turned his back to me, facing the portal. With a single long stride, he stepped into it, vanishing inside.

"You made the wrong choice," Maya whispered, her voice barely audible.

"Be mad at me later," I snapped back. I placed my hand on her side and attempted to heal anything I could. A series of painful stabs hit my side, and I grunted, though I managed to help her to her feet.

Ian's Venators were closing in, as the new sound of running footsteps echoed off the walls as we helped each other wobble forward.

The portal loomed high over our heads as we stepped up to it.

"To Highmoore?" I asked. She nodded weakly, though her eyes showed the same fiery intensity as when I first met her.

"To Highmoore," I repeated, drawing a deep breath as the footsteps grew in volume around us.

To my new home, I hoped. Blowing the breath out, Maya and I stepped into the black abyss of the portal.

Chapter Thirteen

The best way I can describe stepping into a portal is what I imagine jumping out of a plane would be like —I've never done that, either. I felt weightless as I floated through twisting colors that swirled around me, entangling with each other to create dazzling displays, like skydiving through a kaleidoscope. It was a sensory overload, filling my eyes, ears, and nose with floods of everything, and yet nothing at all. It took a lifetime, but it was over in an instant.

The portal deposited us in a chaotic city square. People scurried around, either to or from the middle of the square, where I now stood, helping to keep Maya upright. Buildings marked the edges, each illuminated by what looked like modern lights contrasting against the night sky, which hovered like a black blanket, any shapes or forms of stars blocked by the city lights.

The portal that had thrown us into this foreign city had dissolved behind us. The closest onlookers took notice of us, leading to shouts and the sudden slow of movement as everyone noted our arrival. A group of at least fifteen men and women of all ages crept closer to us, their swords drawn and pointed at me. I tried to form Frostbite, but the buzz on my finger was gone, reminding me of the trade I'd made, which the girl I was helping stand was not happy about.

A familiar voice sounded above the rest, and she soon came shoving through the group with the swords, dragging a little dark-haired boy behind her. They pushed the last few out of her way, reaching the center and us. The little boy wrapped around my waist. I hugged back with my free hand.

"What happened to her?" Lucinda asked.

Murmurs grew once the crowd realized what was going on. I heard a few say "Maledictus" through the rest of the hum, followed by anyone who wasn't already to turn and look as well. Everyone's attention was on me, and already it was making my skin crawl.

"Jaden!" Lucinda said sharply, jarring me back.

"Vincent," I said.

"What about him? Where is he?"

Maya groaned as Lucinda helped shoulder her, taking the half of her that wasn't wrapped around my neck. "He was working for Ian," she whispered.

"He tried to get me to join him; kill me when I said no," I added.

She spouted off some words in Latin. Based on how she said them, I can only assume she wasn't wishing him the best.

"Is he alive?"

"Yeah, but he got away through the portal."

Lucinda grabbed my hand, looking at each finger. "And where is the ring?" she asked, her eyes narrowing.

I ripped my hand away as Maya coughed, then said, "He traded it for me. I told him not to."

"Yeah, my bad," I said, under my breath.

"It's not good," Lucinda said, somehow hearing me. "The Queen won't be thrilled by the news, but she's beyond eager to see you. She's been waiting for fifteen years. Best you don't make her wait any longer." Then she shouted, "Can I get a Medela?"

A woman stepped through those with swords now, splitting between a girl with auburn hair and a dark-haired guy with similar facial features, both who looked to be about my age. The crowd let her through, but never took their eyes off me.

The woman reached us, looking fondly at Maya, before placing a hand on her head. She healed her while I studied her face. Her features were strikingly similar to the girl she healed, and I wondered if it was her mother. The woman removed her hand as Maya took a deep breath, able to stand on her own.

"Thank you, Willow," Lucinda said. The woman smiled at her before returning to the crowd.

The same crowd parted as we made our way through it. All eyes were on us, specifically me. I wanted to disappear, but I forced myself to stand tall, focusing my attention on Ollie, holding his hand and navigating the crowd. A few members separated themselves, falling in behind us and following as we made our way out of the square.

We weaved through lit roads made of stone and other rocky materials. More shops lined the streets, though they sat undisturbed in the nighttime hour. Even without the daylight, I could feel the brilliance of each building, as if the medieval times met the future. I could only imagine the city in the daylight.

We rounded a row of shops onto another main road. That's

when I saw it for the first time: a grand castle, if you could call it that, over-watching the rest of the city. Lights radiated from every square inch of the structure, glistening into the dark night sky above. It sat on a hill, the highest point in the sleeping city, tending to the rest of the metropolis like a mother hen tends to her chicks.

"That's Castle Dawnburn," Maya said. I repeated the name. "The sun rises behind it, making it look like it's on fire every morning. It's very pretty."

It didn't take us long to reach the base of the steps that led up to its massive front doors. A pair of guards, each wearing some type of leather armor and army boots over jeans and a shirt completed the modern medieval look as they stepped aside to let us climb. As we reached the landing, Lucinda turned us around to look over the city.

Ollie let go of my hand, his amber eyes sparkling as the lights twinkled from the massive expanse of the city below.

Maya shuffled around Lucinda to stand next to me. "This is it," she said, a sense of pride in her voice.

"This is home," I said, trying to convince myself.

"This is the other side of the portal. Welcome home, Maledictus."

Chapter Fourteen

The massive front doors swung open behind us, stealing my attention from the city. Lucinda set a hand on my and Maya's shoulders, steering us into and through the opening, where a crowd of people awaited us. Voices rose and bounced off the glistening stone walls, which were polished smooth, way fancier than even anything in the Edwards' house.

Those in the castle came to greet us, a mix of English and agitated Latin surrounding and showering down on us. Maya was separated from me, sets of hands pulling her away and down a hallway. She looked back and yelled at me, but it was lost in the sea of voices.

Eventually, the number of those in the entrance dwindled as people were dismissed by an unseen leader. I'd grabbed hold of Ollie subconsciously, just now realizing the firm grip on his arm. I relaxed my hand, scanning those remaining in the hall, as well as the artwork and other decorations that lined the grand entryway.

A woman stepped forward, and my heart skipped a beat. The sparkle in her eyes, the gentle smile; it was the woman I'd seen two times before: My mother. A weird urge to go to her, wrap myself in her arms and never let go washed over me, but I pushed it aside, forcing my feet to stay planted.

Only five of us remained in the hall. Lucinda and Ollie to either side of me, Queen Iris in front, and a younger woman next to her, who could barely contain her excitement at being a part of the moment.

Iris moved closer, now just a foot in front of me, looking up into my eyes with nothing but pure love. "My little boy," she said, a tear dropping down her cheek. "You do not know how often I've dreamed of this moment."

I smiled but couldn't think of anything to say.

"Jaden, hug your mother," Lucinda scolded.

The woman laughed across from me, wiping away the tears as she did. "Give him time, Lucinda. He's still in shock." She ruffled my hair. "Oh, you look just like your father. I'm so sorry you two never met, and I'm sorry we're just now meeting. Come with me. I want to hear all about your life."

She turned to the other woman. "Brooke, this is my son, Jaden. Jaden, this is Brooke. She's my *adiutor*, my assistant. I don't know what I'd do without her."

Brooke smiled at me, then thanked my mother for the compliment. "It's my honor, ma'am. Is there anything you need? The Council Hall is open, as you requested."

"Will you take the little one here and show him to the Dawnburn guestroom?" she asked, gesturing toward Ollie.

I shook my head. "He's coming with us."

Mom smiled, turning back to Brooke. "Very well. Make sure

both his and Jaden's rooms are ready for them." Brooke gave a quick bow before turning and hurrying down the hallway they had taken Maya.

Lucinda joined my mother, talking with her quietly as they led us past the hall the others had gone, continuing straight and deeper into the castle. Ollie walked beside me, his head twisting and turning, a giant smile plastered to his face, awed by his new surroundings. I couldn't help but smile as he pointed to every-thing, saying, "Look at that!"

We turned down hallway after hallway, each one grander than the last, before reaching our destination. Queen Iris entered a room as a pair of guards stepped aside, opening a pair of heavyset doors, reclaiming their place once they closed them behind us. The Council Hall, as Brooke had referred to it, looked more like a giant chapel than a meeting room. Where there would've been pews, instead, was mostly empty space on the sides of the room, as only a single, enormous, rectangular table filled the space in the middle of the room. Plush chairs lined the table, though only on one end. I counted only seven chairs, leaving at least thirty feet of empty table.

Iris and Lucinda took two of the chairs, gesturing for Ollie and me to take two on the other side of the table. I sat, scanning the rest of the room, giving myself time to take it all in. Quartz pillars extended to the high ceiling, shimmering as brightly as the outside of the castle had, and I realized the entire castle was made of the expensive stone.

I felt eyes on me, and I brought my gaze down to match my mother's, who stared at me with a gentle smile. I gave an uneasy smile back. Although we had only just met after fifteen years, she seemed to already truly care about me, and that would take some getting used to.

Her face suddenly turned to surprise, followed by what looked like slight embarrassment. "You must be starving! Please forgive me, I haven't been a mother for fifteen years. I'm a little out of practice."

She grabbed at the necklace she wore, fiddling with the square pendant. "What would you like? We can make anything, and it will be better than anything you've had on Earth, from what Lucinda tells me."

I wasn't hungry and wouldn't be eating soon, especially after everything that had occurred in the past few hours. I shook my head and politely declined.

"What about for the little guy?" she asked, then said, "I'm sorry. I never got his name."

"My name is Oliver, but everyone calls me Ollie!"

"Well, Ollie, do *you* want anything to eat?"

"No, thank you."

"Such manners! Tell me, Jaden, how do you two know each other?"

I told her how we met in a foster home and had become close before being adopted into the same family, technically becoming brothers. It was a long story, but she listened intently, like I always imagined a mother would. She responded by telling us he was welcome to live with us in the castle, making a joke about Lucinda and Maya being too good at their jobs, returning with two sons instead of one. Then she turned to Ollie.

"Well, Oliver, my name is Iris. I'm Jaden's mom. Seeing as you two are brothers, that makes me your mom now, too."

"But Rose is my mom," Ollie said, confusion on his face.

"She is, but she's asked that I help her be your mom, since she isn't able to see you as much anymore."

He still looked confused but answered "Okay" before yawning.

"We should get you boys to bed. I imagine you've both had a few long days, and I can't wait to hear about them tomorrow. Lucinda, will you take Oliver to his room? I'll show Jaden to his."

I said goodnight to Lucinda and Ollie, who looked reluctant to leave me. But he had developed a trust in the older woman far faster than I had and allowed her to lead him out of the large room and down a long hallway softly lit at the late hour.

I walked beside my mother, not far behind them. She wrapped her arm around the back of my neck, resting her hand on my shoulder. I tensed up, and she smiled, removing her arm. I immediately felt bad. She was my mom, after all.

"I understand," she said, reading my mind. "You don't know me. You've grown up not knowing your parents, and there's a pit in my heart knowing that. But as your mother, I will do my best to make up for all the time lost."

She stopped us in front of a thick wooden door. "This is your room. Mine is just down the hall, if you need anything." She pointed to the end of the hall, where two large doors were shut. "I'm so glad you're home, Jaden. Try to get some sleep. Tomorrow is a big day. There're many people who can't wait to meet you."

She smiled goodnight, opening the door. "Goodnight, honey."

* * *

194

The door closed behind me, leaving me alone in my new room. The lights were off, but beams of light shined through a bank of windows on the opposite side. A flat-panel glass light switch hung on the wall. I slid my fingers up it; the lights grew in brightness. I turned them back down, enough for me to see my way around.

The room itself was a large square, the same shiny stone making up the walls and floor. A bed, larger than all the beds I've slept on in my life combined, sat on the side wall, facing out and into the room. A wooden desk sat in front of the bank of windows, the view outside overlooking the city. Next to the desk was a full-size mirror that stretched from the floor to well over my head. An open door in the wall away from the bed led to my own bathroom. My *own* bathroom. I'd grown up sharing the same bathroom with too many kids to count, and now I could use my own, built into my *own* room. I chuckled at the absurdity of the room; it reminded me of a fancy New York apartment you'd see on TV.

Two sets of clothes sat on the edge of the bed, meticulously folded. One set contained a simple Army green shirt and a pair of black shorts, which I put in the bathroom. I didn't know if everyone wore Earth-like clothes or if they had just given me some, but either way, I appreciated it. I put the other set on the desk, ready for the morning.

After removing them from my pocket, I stashed the two social security cards in a drawer before unhooking Noah's dagger from my ankle, placing it and its sheath on the desk, too. I started for the bathroom, but stopped, instead picking up the weapon again. The metal glimmered, even in the low light. My fingers ran the length of the blade, both the smooth flat surfaces and the jagged edge. Not having my own stuff growing up, I wasn't much of a sentimental kid, but this knife meant something now. I'd survived everything that had been thrown at me, literally including the dagger in my hands. Without the ring, it had become my primary defense. I sighed, sheathed the dagger, and headed for what appeared to be the shower.

* * *

It might've been the longest shower I've ever taken. It had been days since my last, and trust me, if you had the misfortune of being close enough to get a whiff of me, you'd have told me to shower again.

I dressed in the shorts, but before I put on the shirt, I stepped back into my bedroom and in front of the mirror. My eyes traced their way down my body, taking in every new and old scar, scrape, or bruise, starting with the days-old one on my temple from Noah and the dagger. A small ridge was all that remained from the cut I'd gotten from the flying rock in the train station, though my ribs looked like I'd just lost a boxing match, as scrapes crisscrossed over deeper brown bruises. They ached when I breathed deep, but they would heal eventually.

Though it was hidden by the shorts, the slash I'd taken from the skelecat claw stung. I shook my head; the cut reminding me just how many times I should've died the last few days. *You're not the same kid you once were.*

My eyes shifted to the lengthy scar on my right forearm and the worst night of my life, both at the Alvarez house and in general, when a piece of shattered glass tore its way through the skin and muscle, leaving a three-inch gash that had taken twelve-year-old me being driven to a hospital to stop the bleeding.

Learn to dance, Jaden. Learn to dance and those pesky rain showers are only water for the flowers.

I wondered if Mr. Alvarez would be proud of me.

I stared hard into the mirror. The glowing eyes were gone, replaced by a vibrant blue iris, one that Rose would've been even more jealous of.

I'm home, I tried to convince myself.

A knock on the door interrupted me. Facing the sound, I only half expected Ian, Esham, or even Noah to enter and attempt to rid Arrortha of Maledictus. Instead, a man, I assumed one of the castle guards, poked his head in.

"You Jaden?" he asked.

"Yeah."

He opened the door wider, and Ollie barged past. The man closed the door behind him. I smiled as Ollie threw down the sheets of the bed, crawling into it before covering himself.

At least he showered, I thought, his still wet hair poking over the top of the covers.

I turned back to the mirror one last time, but the exhaustion I'd been pushing away washed over me. I put on the shirt; the bruises reminding me of their presence.

The lights shut off as I swiped down on the wall remote before joining Ollie in bed. I worried sleeping would be difficult, but the thick, fluffy mattress consumed me as I laid down, and sleep gripped me within minutes.

15

The sun was filtering its way through the windows of my room before I opened my eyes again. Outside of the few rays, the room was dark and quiet. Ollie breathed softly next to me, still fast asleep. I rubbed my face, crawling out of bed to not wake him up. I passed the desk in front of the windows, stopping to look out. A few clouds hung low over the outskirts of the city, burning away from the rising sun. My window faced a different direction than the front of the castle, letting me see only the side of the city, as well as a range of rolling green hills and taller mountains beyond. It was definitely different from waking up to the morning skyline in DC. I grabbed the set of clothes from the desk and headed for the shower.

After a quick one, I exited the bathroom dressed in dark gray athletic pants and a black T-shirt, throwing my sweatshirt over the top.

Ollie sat awake in bed, the mop of black hair on his head a tangled mess. He looked at me with a *where am I?* look, but the pieces clicked into place, and without a word he got out of bed, walked past me, and into the bathroom.

I grabbed my dagger, attaching it to my leg as Ollie walked out of the bathroom at the same time there was a knock on the door. We answered it together to see Brooke standing there, a smile on her face.

"Good morning, boys! Queen Iris has asked me to show you to the dining area."

We followed her down the hall, stopping at Ollie's room so he could change. Brooke attempted to make small talk with me while we waited, but after discovering how bad I was at it, we waited in silence.

Ollie rejoined us a few minutes later, and Brooke led us down the hall, through a set of grand double doors, and into a dining room. I was expecting a giant room filled with tables and people, but this one was so... normal. A chandelier hung from the ceiling, though it was unlit; a row of windows were opened, allowing sunlight and fresh air to provide light to the room. A single, large table adorned the center, with only one occupant enjoying the large spread of food laid out buffet-style in the center.

We were shown seats across from the diner and introduced to him; an old, plump man named Cassius Cole. Cassius grunted an annoyed greeting at us, focusing his attention back on his plate of eggs, which must be universal, and his cup of steaming liquid, which smelled of coffee.

Brooke ignored the lack of greeting, telling us to "help yourselves to anything on the table." Then she said something that caught my attention. "Maya will be here shortly to show you around the kingdom."

"She's alive?" I asked, my pulse quickening. *Of course she's alive, you idiot. She walked into the castle with you.*

"Very much so, thanks to you. I've got other business to attend to, but you guys eat, and she will be here any second to come and get you. I'm sure Cassius here will be *more* than willing to help you if you need it."

Cassius didn't acknowledge her, or us, instead devouring everything on his plate. Brooke gave him a testy smile before exiting the room. I turned my attention to the spread of food. Some of it looked like it had come through the portal with us:

eggs, a muffin, a stack of pancakes. Some dishes; however, I'd never seen before. As I scanned my options, Cassius cleared his throat.

"So, you're the queen's son?"

His voice was gravelly, like he had been smoking since he was ten. A white beard made its way around his round face, though he looked more like an angry grandpa than Santa Claus.

I nodded a response, looking at a silver tray on which a single muffin sat.

"Hmph. You may be Maledictus, but if you touch that muffin, I will stab you with a fork."

Was this dude serious?

I glanced at him, but his face showed no signs of joking, and he gripped the utensil he had used for his eggs. As much as I wanted to, I decided not to test his fork stabbing abilities, instead choosing some meat that looked like sausage. Ollie's plate was still empty, his stare aimed at the muffin. I glanced back at the big man, who was still locked in on me, oblivious to his muffin's real threat.

Ollie's shoulder shot past me, his hand grabbing the pastry, pulling it back to his chest, clutching it tightly. I reached for the dagger; I could have it out and pressed against this guy's throat way before he could get close to my brother.

Instead, Cassius sat back in his chair, his stomach bouncing as he let out a deep laugh. He stood, pointing to Ollie as he headed for the door.

"You better watch out for that little one. He may get you into more trouble than you can handle, Maledictus."

He continued through the door, still laughing as it swung shut. Ollie tore off pieces as he watched him go, then turned to me, a smile stretching from ear to ear. I laughed with him, finishing the rest of the sausage.

The doors swung open a few minutes later as Maya walked in.

"How was your first night?" she asked, breezing past us and grabbing a scone from the table.

"Good," Ollie and I said in unison.

"Good. Are you done eating? Queen Iris wanted to see you before I showed you around."

We nodded, following her out of the dining room. The castle was still a maze to me, and after a few turns, I was totally lost again.

Eventually, we came to a crowded hallway. People walked both ways, entering and exiting rooms, each one moving with a purpose. Maya joined the pace as Ollie and I kept up, ignoring the odd looks from others as we passed.

A cluster of people were gathered at the end of the hall. As we approached, my mother stepped out from the middle, greeting us with a friendly smile.

"How'd you boys sleep?"

We gave a distracted "Good," watching the busy hallway as the castle occupants went about their business.

She put a hand on my shoulder, bringing me back to focusing on her. "I wish I could go with you, but I am a bit busy here. Go with Maya, and when you get back, I promise I will answer any questions you have."

She gave us a hug, thanked Maya for taking us, and then melted back into the group.

* * *

We started the tour in the castle. Maya led us down about twenty hallways, pointing out room after room, most of which I forgot by the time we moved on to the next one. Eventually, we found parts of the castle that did interest me. Maya led us into a massive, but dark room, until she used a remote on the wall to bring up the lights.

The first thing I saw was the giant chair at the far end of the room. Polished stone had been sculpted into a magnificent, elegant throne. Designs were carved into the stone, ending in a spired top. I pictured my mother ruling over the kingdom, her gentle but firm smile powerful yet inviting.

After the throne room, we went to the castle armory. Hundreds of swords of varying lengths and shapes hung on the walls or sat on racks. A few guards sorted and polished helmets, chest plates, and other armor pieces into neat piles, making them ready for action whenever they were needed. Ollie stared in wonder at every item in the room, and wasn't thrilled when Maya said it was time to keep moving.

"When do I get my sword?" I asked Maya.

She looked at me incredulously. "You won't get one of these. You'll forge your own. I'll show you where later."

We snaked down more halls from the armory, ending up in the same meeting room from the night before.

"This," Maya said, opening the door to the Council Hall, "is where the most important meetings in Highmoore take place. The Council of Powers meets here once a month at least, more if needed."

"Council of Powers?"

"Glacies, Ferrum, Crescere, all have a representative. It's like your government on Earth… I think. Each power is represented by one person, and they work together to make sure Arrortha is safe for all powers."

"Including Desolate?"

"Yes. I know we told you that most of them moved away and are on Ian's side, but those who aren't are still represented. Queen Iris actually added the Desolate representative after she took over."

A few minutes later, we stood on the same landing we had the previous night. The sun had burned away all the remaining clouds, radiating down on the city.

"Is that the same sun as Earth?" I asked, shielding it with my hand.

Maya shrugged. "As far as we're concerned. Look, there is a lot of history about this place that you'll learn, but even more that *we* don't know. All we have to go off of are books and journals written by people who just 'woke up here.'" She made finger quotes as she spoke.

"Woke up in Arrortha?"

She nodded. "No memory of where they came from, only this place. The one thing they do know is the destruction that took place here. They think there was a giant war before they got here. Castle Dawnburn was the only building not nearly or completely destroyed in Highmoore. They rebuilt the city around the castle."

I looked back over the kingdom, sparkling in the morning light. Most, if not all the buildings, seemed to be made of the same polished quartz as the castle, most of them being either one or two-story, barring the major exception of a massive domed building that looked like a football stadium, just to the side of the city center. I wondered how I could've missed it last night.

Overall, the kingdom was much smaller than any major city I'd been to in the last couple days on Earth, but what it lacked in size, it made up for in beauty. Beyond the city, the same mountains stretched off into the distance. Something about the name didn't make sense to me.

Maya started down the steps, but I stopped her. "Wait." She turned back, her head tilted to the side. "Dawnburn isn't Latin. Is Highmoore Latin?"

"No, it's the last name of one of the people who wrote the history books."

"Are the books written in Latin?"

"Not the oldest ones. Those are in some weird version of English. The more recent ones are in Latin."

The wheels in my head started spinning; Maya smiled as I pieced things together.

"They came from Earth and knew English? Why did they learn Latin?"

"It's the only language Krera spoke, and she tends to get her way. Don't worry, she's gotten pretty good at English by now," she said, continuing down the steps.

We made our way into the city, past the same rows of businesses, though they were open now, their advertisements and shop workers calling out to anyone passing by, including us. Most of the shops sold services. Medela shops offered to heal any aches or pains. Crescere markets sold many agricultural crops, as well as clothing and other items made from plants. The smell of fresh-baked bread accompanied these shops, and even after just having breakfast, the aroma teased my stomach. Maya pointed out Ferrum shops, each displaying swords, axes, and other spiky objects. Signs offered more details on each weapon, but most were written in Latin, leaving me to guess what they said.

At one shop, a large, muscular, bearded man leaned against a display of swords. He looked more menacing than any of the weapons, but Maya strolled up to him, almost breaking into a jog.

"Theo!"

The big man's face lit up as he saw her. "My favorite Medela returns! I've been worried sick about you."

Maya jumped into his arms. He caught her, squeezing her tight like his favorite child.

Once he set her down, she introduced me. "Theo, this is Jaden."

"Maledictus, yes. You're the talk of the town."

I gave him a half-smile as I shook his hand, but said nothing.

Maya continued. "I got him back in one piece, Theo! Well, he got me back in one, but I won't tell if you don't."

"I wouldn't dare," he said, grinning.

"Jaden, Theo is going to help you make your own sword. He's the best in the town, and your mother asked for him specifically."

"And I am honored. I'm sure you're busy trying to keep up with her, but when you're ready, I've got some designs we can go over."

I agreed, Maya said her goodbyes, and we continued on into the city. The deeper we got, the more I realized how normal, yet different, everything was.

"Why does it look like a modern medieval city?"

She laughed, then answered. "Like I said before, there's a lot we don't know about this place. What we know is that most of

Highmoore has kept its design, just modernized with time, just as any Earth city."

It made sense, I guess.

We had almost made it to the city center, but most everyone knew Maledictus had arrived last night, and word was spreading fast he was out and about now. Windows were opened, curtains drawn, and people stepped outside, all attempting to see the kid who had been cursed at birth.

Once one person spotted me, the whole kingdom had. Everyone watched the three of us pass by. It was a living nightmare. Some approached us, greeting and welcoming me home, expressing their awe at the queen's son's return. But for every supporter, there was at least one person who scowled, not hiding their dislike that I was here. No one dared attack us, but I still forced Ollie to walk between me and Maya, who kept an eye on everyone as well.

We arrived in the city square, which in the daytime was a thriving market. Individual booths were arranged in rows, each displaying products. Shouting, some in Latin, some in English, bathed the square in sound. People milled about, bartering with shop owners or sampling foods. Though I'd never been to one, it was what I pictured a farmer's market to be like.

A familiar face scanned a couple booths before spotting us. Lucinda's face softened, and she stuck an arm out to accept a hug from Ollie, her staff in the other.

"Is it okay if he goes with you?" Maya asked. "I'm going to show Jaden the testing grounds."

Lucinda looked at Ollie. "Would you like to help me get ingredients for supper?"

Ollie grinned and nodded.

"He will be fine with me. Be careful with him, Maya. You know how hunters are."

"I do," Maya said, her face hardening, almost surely thinking of Vincent.

She snapped out of it, telling me to follow her as we made our way through the close to one hundred people in the square that had stopped their shopping, now very aware that Maledictus was among them.

We left the market, taking a side street that avoided a majority of the crowds, where we walked for a minute or two. After ducking between two Medela shops, Maya stopped in the middle of the stone street, looking up at the grand stadium in front of us.

"This is the testing grounds?" I asked.

The arena, like the other buildings, sparkled in the morning sun.

Maya nodded. "That's what the Venators called it, so most went with it. You can call it the arena or the training center, but it's more like a school for the powers. This will be your favorite place in Highmoore, so let's go."

The sound of clanging metal and yelling was the first thing I noticed when we entered the building, though I couldn't see anything but the hallway we were in. The second was the smell. An acrid mix of burning and body odor lingered in the air, reminding me just slightly of the Alvarez house after we were given time outside.

We turned right, passing doors on either side of the long hall, but Maya ushered me past them. She turned us left, down a hallway that led deeper into the building. A large set of iron doors stood tall at the end of the hall, but we turned and headed up a staircase before reaching them. We went up about thirty feet until the stairs opened to an elevated concrete track-like road that circled the inside of the building. Railings lined both sides, preventing falling, but allowing me to look over both sides.

"This is the viewing area," Maya said, spreading her arms, motioning to the track. "People can come at any time and watch the training, but they must do it from up here if they're not taking part in it. You'll be training below way more than you'll be up here."

We walked around the viewing area while Maya explained the layout.

"There is one main arena surrounded by four practice fields. This is what we call the 'shared field,'" she said, pointing down to a rectangular concrete slab below, the back of which pressed against the arena wall. "Desolate, Ferrum, and Medela share it. It's used mostly by Ferrums to try out new weapons."

Below us, people of all ages worked with swords and other weapons while others watched, offering tips. An archery range sat mostly unoccupied near the back wall, used by a group of younger kids watching an older woman give a demonstration on Medela powers.

We continued around the track, coming up to the next practice area, which was separated from the shared field by a shiny rock wall that rose all the way to the viewing area, preventing the fields from seeing each other.

"This is the Crescere area. It's usually the busiest."

Just as she had said, a ton of people occupied the space, using it efficiently. Multiple gardens were surrounded by kids and adults alike, some growing different crops, while others tried to stop a group of teenage troublemakers who ran around the different gardens, swiping their hands and removing the plants that others had grown. A large climbing wall loomed on the side of the gardens. Kids older than me went three at a time, creating and using ivy and other vine-like plants as they raced to the top. Beside them, a young kid around Ollie's age ran with a giant smile, avoiding the same plants shot at him by a herd of others, attempting to rope him like a cow.

Maya ushered me on before the kid got caught, moving to the third practice field. "This one is for Lapis. Watch for flying objects."

I tentatively peeked over the edge. This area was much more organized than the Crescere one, with far fewer people, most of them around twenty years old. They were in line, taking turns racing through an obstacle course. They'd produce stones to climb on, defend themselves, or even shoot at targets along the way. The stones would shatter, sending shards everywhere, adding another dangerous element to the course. Those not involved in the training practiced creating shields, blocking the swinging stick of an older attacker before creating their own makeshift weapon out of sharpened stone, stabbing past the instructor, and into a target the size of a human. So far, the Lapis was the most well-trained power.

Before I could move to the final practice field, Maya turned me toward the middle of the arena, where a gigantic, open, circular area was broken up by different styles of obstacles that could be used as cover or obstructions. The middle area was empty at the moment.

"That is the true hunting grounds," she said. "The *Iudicium venationes,* or trial hunts, are hosted here. They're a big deal, usually happen a couple times a month. People come from all over the city to watch."

"What are they?"

"It's mainly a test for the Venators, to practice what they've learned. It's usually against each other, but sometimes an unlucky Glacies is appointed the victim, since they usually put up the best fight. All players are given dulled weapons, and the Venators do what they're trained to do, while the hunted person or persons survive as long as they can."

"They get killed?" I asked, appalled at the barbaric game.

"Oh, no! There are Medela everywhere in the arena, and they immediately heal anyone who is wounded. They might be in pain for a bit, but nobody has ever died."

She turned and walked to the final practice field. "This, Jaden, is the Glacies area. While you could technically learn in any practice area, this will be where you train."

The Glacies field was by far the least populated. A few young kids climbed a wall by freezing their hands and feet while adults watched. A woman practiced firing snowballs at moving targets next to the wall, ducking and rolling after each throw as imaginary ones were fired back at her.

The other two occupants were locked in a heated battle. The auburn-haired girl from last night held a sword, swinging and blocking against a boy about my age. The guy held only a small knife, the tip of the blade barely visible at a distance. He weaved around her sword, mostly dodging, but with an unbelievable smoothness, narrowing the distance between their bodies.

The Glacies power infiltrated my mind, putting me in his role. My brain dodged and ducked with him, predicting his moves as if they were my own. My mind was part of the fight from up here, my thoughts the same as if I was the kid avoiding the girl's sword.

The guy closed the gap, dipping under a swing before turning his body sideways, gliding past the girl who realized her mistake too late. The blade of the knife was up against her throat before she could move.

After a quick second, he removed the knife, stepping back in front of her. She said something I couldn't hear, motioning with her sword, replicating one of the moves she had attempted. He nodded at her, confirming her suspicion. He took another step back, and they started their battle again.

"Who are they?" I asked Maya, still watching the pair.

"They're the Hamilton twins. The girl's name is Quinn. The guy is Khyden. Both have Glacies power. They've been training here since they were twelve, so three years now. The hunters have been trying to recruit Khyden since he stepped in here the first day after getting his power and beat half of the Glacies with no practice. Now that he's fifteen and has years of experience, they're trying even harder, but he won't do it. I think he'd be an amazing private hunter for your mother. You two are destined to be friends if you'd ever talk to each other. He doesn't say much, kind of like you. But"—she pointed at him as he avoided the pointy end of his sister's sword—"if there is one person in this building who can give you an actual fight, it's Ky."

She watched the fight continue, a smile on her face. I was the last person to know *anything* about dating, but I was beginning to think Maya had a crush this Khyden guy.

I wonder how she feels about me.

Soon after, Maya took me down to meet them. She strolled

into the Glacies area, rubbing her arms and complaining about how "You ice people always keep it so cold in here."

She called out to them, distracting Quinn as she countered an attack from her brother, who ended up next to her, the knife inches away from her throat again.

"*Damnare,* Maya! Do you know how hard I worked to finally counter that move? I had him right where I wanted him."

Khyden smirked next to her, as if he had had something else planned.

Quinn sighed. "What is it?" she asked.

Her auburn hair ran down past her shoulders, bunched together from the exertion, covering parts of a necklace that ducked beneath her shirt. Green eyes glowered at Maya under thick, furrowed eyebrows. Right away, I could tell she was not the type to mess around with.

"Sorry to interrupt. It really did look like you had him this time! There's someone I want you to meet. This is Jaden Frost."

Quinn nodded, sheathing her sword and crossing her arms in front of her. "The queen's son. I'd heard you made it back, figured Maya would bring you here soon enough. Anyway, I'm Quinn. This is my twin brother, Khyden."

Khyden nodded slightly, hanging his knife on a small hook, which sat on top of an odd square on the silver chain he wore, the rest of the knife hanging freely down his chest. A large circle was cut out of the end of the thin grip for his index finger, while grooves had been molded for the rest of them. The short blade of the weapon curved to the side until it ended in a sharp-looking tip. I'd seen knives like it in video games before, but I couldn't remember what it was called.

"Are you guys really twins?" I asked, doubting what Maya had said earlier.

Quinn smiled, as if she got that question often. "Yes, we really are. Ky here was lucky enough to get Mom's eyes and her tan skin, while all I got was Dad's eyebrows and his pastiness. Clearly, I'm not jealous."

"Definitely not," I said, which got a laugh from the group.

Then Quinn's eyes narrowed. "I've heard rumors about what you're supposed to be able to do. Have all the powers, be the best of the best. You want a turn against Ky? Nobody else here can beat him, except for a few of the elite Glacies Venators, and even then, it's only half the time."

"Those guys aren't Maledictus," Khyden said, speaking for the first time. His voice was much softer than I expected. It was warmer, gentler.

He shifted on his feet, standing straight up, at least a couple of inches taller than me. Short, dark-colored hair hung over his forehead, ending just an inch shy of eyes that were an impossibly deep shade of brown. They were magnetic, a mask of softness that attempted to hide the fiery warrior behind them. I could now see why Maya had a crush.

"As much as everyone would love that, right now he's got somewhere else he needs to be," Maya said.

We said our goodbyes, and as the Hamilton twins resumed training, Maya led me out of the arena and onto the main road, heading back toward the castle.

"Where else do I have to go?"

"You remember the Council of Powers, and how they meet once a month, or whenever they feel they need to? Well, they're meeting this afternoon, and they've specifically requested your attendance."

16

We stood outside of the Council Hall doors shortly after. Two guards stepped aside to let me in, closing the gap after I'd passed. I looked back between them at Maya, who gave me a confident nod, just as the heavy doors swung shut with a thud.

I was back inside the massive room, but this time, the long table was occupied. Seven people sat on the far side of the table, comically far away from the entrance doors. Most I didn't recognize, though Lucinda flanked my mother, who sat at the head of the table, an open chair next to her. She beckoned me toward it, where I sat, facing the rest of the table.

"Where's Ollie?" I whispered to Lucinda.

"In the kitchen, helping the cooks make dinner."

Queen Iris stood, ending our conversation. She put her hands on the table, addressing everyone in the room. "I would like to know why the council has requested my son's presence."

An older, dark-skinned guy with a baritone voice answered her. "With all due respect, Your Highness, we felt it was best if he was aware of the circumstances regarding Ian and was at least present for the decisions. He is Maledictus, after all."

"He's fifteen, Arthur." She looked at Lucinda. "And you agree with this decision?"

"Actually, ma'am, it was my idea."

Queen Iris took a deep breath, taking a moment to gather herself before continuing. "Very well. Who wants to start?"

A beautiful woman around my mother's age said, "I've asked

Bryce Delacroix to attend as well. As head Venator, I feel he can give us insight into what Ian might do next."

A middle-aged man with muscular arms nodded to the council, but before he could speak, the same gravelly voice that had threatened to stab me over a muffin spoke first.

"Perhaps there are other hunters who might have better knowledge of Ian's motives?"

"What does that mean?" Bryce asked, his eyes narrowing at the older man across the table.

"How can we be certain there aren't more Venators, even trainees, who are aligned with Ian? Perhaps Vincent's own trainer? If Mr. Delacroix here isn't aware of who he is sending after your son, Maledictus, no less, can we be certain he is aware of the alliance of all his members?"

The Venator's jaw flexed, but he cooled himself before he spoke. "What Vincent did has no reflection on the rest of us, Cassius. And I can assure you, personal history has no bias in this situation. If I recall correctly, it was one of your Ferrums who placed the ability on his ax for that mission. Are you certain they weren't working together?"

The two men shot daggers at one another.

"Gentlemen!" Lucinda snapped from her seat, drawing stares from both men. She returned the coldness to each before turning to the queen. "Ma'am, we are concerned about the growing support for Ian within Highmoore. And, through no fault of his own, it feels as if Jaden's arrival has sent waves through the city."

My mother nodded, agreeing with her assessment. "Bryce, what do you expect Ian's next move to be?"

"He will look to capitalize on the effect Maledictus' arrival has caused."

"Meaning?"

"Depending on how effective he has been at gaining an army, there is a possibility of an attack within the next few days. I don't believe it would be one directed at the entire city, but instead one at you, or him," he said, pointing at me. "If he were to... kill Maledictus, he could win the support of those who had not yet chosen a side. Power attracts in Arrortha, and what better way to display power than proving the queen's son wasn't safe? He could have other kingdoms aligned with him shortly after."

"Could killing a fifteen-year-old boy who was just reunited with his mother be seen as an overstep, losing him support?" asked the same woman who had introduced Bryce.

"I'm not sure he would care. Maledictus would still be dead. His goal ever since placing the curse has been ruling Arrortha. He will destroy Highmoore without a second thought to achieve it. We now know he's in possession of the ring, so through past agreements, he is the ruler."

"Most of the kingdoms don't respect a true ruler, much less if they are in possession of the ring. That was due to him, and I don't expect that to change just because he is wearing it now. Our allies still outnumber his," Lucinda said.

Cassius spoke again. "Are we not convinced that sending Maledictus back to Earth won't ease the tensions? I've spoken with Scott." He gestured to a man with graying hair and a trim beard next to him, who stared at the table, avoiding all eye contact. "And he agreed that the neutral Desolates, like himself, would see the move as one toward peace. It could bring them to our side. Plus, Ian could send all the men he wants. It would still take fifteen more years to find him on Earth."

Lucinda shook her head, closing her eyes like a disappointed grandmother.

"Cassius," my mother started, not bothering to hide the anger in her voice. "I met my son last night for the first time since he was only days old. While he's clearly grown into a strong and powerful boy while on Earth, I will *not* be losing him again."

"If we're not willing to ease the tensions, they will continue to rise, and Arrortha will have a war over that child right there."

"We are willing," Arthur said. "Your Highness, the Lapis and Crescere people work hand-in-hand. After discussing with Sierra," he said, gesturing to the beautiful woman across the table from him, "we suggest Highmoore keep to itself. She will support her allies and stay ready, but any aggression from Ian will be seen as just that. We have Searchers in every town nearby. We will know if he's attacking."

This got a few nods from the group. Cassius rolled his eyes, but the group ignored his disdain for the plan.

I listened while the Council discussed further. Eventually, they reached a consensus that Highmoore would help those who requested it, but would otherwise only worry about improving its defenses. Protection would increase around my mother, though nobody thought Ian would dare try something so foolish.

The queen stood, motioning me to follow her. The rest of the council remained seated.

"The council still has more to discuss, but I know you're overwhelmed already," she said, leading me to the door. "I'll see you at dinner, when I want to hear all about the rest of your day."

Back out in the hall, Maya sat on a wooden bench, waiting for me. She perked up as I sat next to her. "How'd that go?"

I shrugged.

"Follow me. I want to show you something I think you'll like."

"I want to check on Ollie first."

We found him in the kitchen, just as Lucinda had said. He followed each cook around as they hustled between stations, throwing in different spices or preparing slabs of meat over flames. He waved at us, but kept his interest in the food, so we exited the kitchen, back into the main hallway.

Maya led me down the main stairs of the castle, turning onto a side path at the base of steps that wound back behind the fortress.

We followed the path for ten minutes as it twisted through a field of grass and bright, multicolored flowers. The breeze shifted, lifting a pleasant scent up from the blossoms all around us.

The path stopped on the edge of a cliff that overlooked a spacious valley below. Mountains lined both sides and much of the distance beyond, past where the valley gave way to the horizon. It was breathtaking, unlike anything I'd seen during my time on Earth.

Sunlight glistened and reflected off distant buildings in the valley, their distance impossible to judge.

"What are those?" I asked, Maya following my pointing finger.

"The buildings? That's Straucka, Highmoore's closest neighbors, and one of our best allies. They're much smaller than we are, but I guess it's reassuring to have them on our side."

We sat in the grass, staring out over the view and enjoying nothing but the sound of the wind as it blew gently over the open land. The thoughts of the field where I trailed the skeleton kept forcing its way to the front of my mind. I did my best to push it aside, but no matter what I tried, it refused to be ignored.

After a few minutes, Maya glanced at me with a soft smile. "How are you doing?"

I turned to look at her. Her hair moved softly with the breeze, and she brushed it out of her face. "What?"

"How are you doing? Since you got here."

I thought about it. "I don't know."

I didn't dare tell her the truth: I was lonely. The entire city knew of my existence, and I'd rarely been alone since I'd arrived, and still, here I was. I was used to being alone; it was peaceful to me. But when I felt alone? That was miserable, and it was mostly all I'd known. Yet there was something about her that seemed to lessen that feeling.

She nodded, but didn't ask anything else, instead turning back to face the view. After a few seconds, I did the same, the quietness retaking the meadow.

At least on the outside. In my head, it was as loud as ever. I wanted to say something else to her, just to keep talking to her, but I didn't know what. It was a curious feeling. I'd never wanted to start a conversation with anyone, and yet I sat there, begging my brain to find any reason to have a connection with this girl I'd only known for days. The thought horrified me. Not that I thought I might have a friend in her, but that I *wanted* one.

In the end, I said nothing, sitting quietly, listening to the grass blow in the wind, too afraid of ruining it.

Chapter Fifteen

There was a party that evening, and I don't mean a small "welcome home" party. My mother threw the largest party I'd ever been to, much less one where I was the guest of honor. I don't know how many people live in Highmoore, but it felt like everyone was there. A grand dining hall that was decorated and packed to the brim with hundreds of castle staff and other citizens of the city. Tables packed full of food and drinks were available to the guests, who milled around and talked and laughed with each other, their voices drowning the sound of music from a few odd stringed instruments playing in the corner.

Ollie and I followed my mother around as she introduced me to many people. I saw a few faces I recognized, such as Maya and Quinn, who talked to each other while Khyden watched the other guests, locking eyes with me briefly before moving on to other party goers. After meeting what felt like everyone in attendance, I was exhausted and had forgotten the names of almost everyone I'd met.

A few guests lingered around when my mom told me to take Ollie to his room and head to bed myself. We didn't argue, and I led Ollie through the castle hallways, only getting lost once.

"Are you going to be okay sleeping in your own room?" I asked him once we stood outside his bedroom. He yawned and nodded, giving me a hug before entering his room and shutting the door behind him.

I found my room, showered, and was in bed twenty minutes later, wiped out. I expected to fall asleep immediately, but after half an hour, I was nowhere near it.

The same three people took turns occupying my thoughts, my mom taking the first shift. I could tell her love for me, but could I love her back the same way, no matter how badly I wanted to? My heart was scared that it knew the answer.

It'll take time, I told myself.

Ian pushed my mother aside, taking the attention for himself. I knew nothing about him, other than what I'd been told. And while it was all bad, he was obviously influential enough to gain support in the kingdom that had to hate him the most. What if I agreed with him, too?

He killed your dad before you could meet him. That should be enough.

Finally, it was the brown-eyed girl who had shown up on my doorstep. What was it about her that intrigued me so much? She'd become the closest thing I'd had to a genuine friend ever, even if it felt like giving a cat a bath to get me to admit it.

Why wasn't I able to say anything in that field?

It took time, but eventually the trio wore me out, and I dropped off to sleep.

* * *

I was jolted awake by the sound of scuffling footsteps well before dawn. I sat up in bed, listening for any repeat sounds, when a stifled scream pierced the darkness. I rocketed out of the covers, moving as fast and quiet as I could to the desk, where I grabbed my dagger, holding it at the ready.

I was barefoot, but I used this to my advantage, making no noise as I slow-walked toward my door, where more shuffling feet could be heard, accompanied by the occasional soft grunt.

The door was twenty feet away when the sounds stopped, as did I. It was dead silent for a second. Two. Three.

The bedroom door flung open as a figure rushed in, dragging a much smaller shadow behind it. As they crossed the threshold to the room, the small figure latched onto the door frame, momentarily halting their movement, before the larger one ripped the little hands free, throwing the smaller figure into my room, where it landed with a whimper.

The door was shut by the large shadow, clearly a man. It scooped up the smaller figure before backing up toward the wall by the door.

The lights suddenly turned on at maximum brightness. I shielded my eyes, shading them with my arm until they had time to adjust. When they did, my stomach dropped.

I was right; the large figure belonged to a man. Not just any man, but the man responsible for so much of what had happened in my life. The man who had cursed me when I was only days old.

Ian stood there, a gigantic sword sheathed on his back, the handle sticking up just over his shoulder.

Shocked, I wondered how he got into the city, through the castle, all the way into my room. Then I saw the ring. Lucinda had said it was the most powerful item in Arrortha. Maybe it did more than make weapons.

After taking in the rest of the scene, my stomach dropped even further, not at the sight of the ring, but at the hand that wore it, which held the grip of a knife, the blade of which pressed against my brother's neck. I didn't care about too many people in my life, but I was getting tired of seeing them with knives pressed against their throats.

Ian looked around the room, smiling and speaking as he did. "My, my. Welcome home, Maledictus. Mind if I call you Jaden?"

I didn't respond, our vivid blue eyes locking.

"Look, I didn't *want* to be holding a knife to the little guy's throat the first time we met. Ideally, you would already be with me, and I wouldn't have to find you here. But plans change, and Vincent told me what you're capable of, so if you think about it, this"—he waved his hand in front of Ollie with the knife still pressured against him—"is kind of your fault. Don't worry, I won't hold a grudge."

"Let him go," I said, trying my best to stay calm.

"Not how it works."

"What do you want?"

"I want you! More than they do, too. They just need you right now because you've got a curse, just like me. You think Lucinda

223

won't hesitate to also throw you aside? Trust me, you're useful to them to stop me, that's it. I, however, want you to rule Arrortha *with* me, and I'm being gracious enough to offer you one last chance to do that, despite you turning down my first ten tries. You just needed to see the place, first. I can get you out of here, and nobody would even know where you went until it was too late."

"You cursed both of us, killed my dad, tried to kill my mom, and forced me to grow up away from here, remember? Why would I trust you?"

"I made you one of the most powerful kids to ever exist, and you're whining about Mommy and Daddy not being by your side growing up? Vincent told me you thought they abandoned you. At least until that Ice Witch told you otherwise."

"Now you want me to betray her? And your entire plan for that is to insult me and hold my brother hostage?"

"Oh, this?" He shifted the knife around Ollie's throat, who had tears streaming down his face.

"No, this is just motivation. You're the great *Maledictus*," he spat. "I just want to see what you can do. Just be mindful."

"Of what?"

"Yourself. Not every loser kid turns out to be the hero they thought they were."

I stepped forward, my voice a low growl. "Let. Him. Go."

The knife was forced deeper into Ollie's neck, a thin line of blood forming under the sharp edge. Ian smiled. "There he is. Last chance, Jaden."

"My brother has nothing to do with this."

"He's not your actual brother!" he yelled, looking back at the door before talking much faster than before. "And he has everything to do with this. Motivation, remember? One way or another, he'll be useful to me."

He took a step back, widening the distance between us, just as the ring on his finger began to glow a ghastly white, dazzling in the already lit room.

"Oh, and Jaden? Do hurry. I try to be accommodating to all my guests, but where we're going is no place for kids."

Going. The ring. How he got into the castle. Most powerful magical item in Arrortha. I put it all together as the ring flashed, lighting the room even brighter. I dropped the dagger and lunged toward the light.

Just as suddenly as the flash had appeared, it disappeared, along with Ian and Ollie. I tumbled to the floor where they had been, fists full of nothing. It was silent for a moment, but the sound of boots from people running in the hall grew louder with each passing second.

I pinched my arm, hoping I was dreaming. But the world didn't change, and I was already conscious. As the pain subsided, the realization kicked in: Ian had just kidnapped my brother.

The door to the bedroom flew open, and swarms of armed guards piled in. Some broke off, creating a barricade around me as the others checked the room, their swords ready for any danger. I sat on the floor, head hung low, not bothering to look at them.

225

Chapter Sixteen

The next morning, I attended my second Council of Powers meeting. I hadn't fallen asleep again last night. Once the guards had made sure there was nobody lurking in my room, I'd been shut in while they searched the rest of the castle. The door was locked, and I spent the entire night lying on the bed, staring at the ceiling until dawn, when I'd been taken straight to the meeting.

They asked me everything they could think of, rapidly firing questions as soon as I arrived, making my mood even worse.

Did he say where he was going? Did he say what his plans were? Why didn't he kill you?

I didn't have an answer to most, instead telling them about his attempts to recruit me again, and how he had gotten madder each time I'd told him no.

"He's gotten much bolder," said the beautiful woman, Sierra, representing the Crescere power. Everyone at the table nodded but me.

"I will send out Searchers as soon as this meeting ends," my mother said, which earned another round of nods, except for Cassius, who rolled his eyes.

Queen Iris sighed. Clearly, she was tired of the old man. I was, too, and I'd only dealt with him twice. "Do you have something you'd like to say, Cassius?"

I don't know why she bothered asking him.

"I do. This council, since its creation, has never met more than twice in two weeks. And now, on the second day since Maledictus' arrival, we are meeting for the second time. I'm sure everyone else in this room is smart enough to see the correlation."

"What's your problem with me?" I blurted out.

"Before you were found and rescued from Earth, we had peace," he said, staring at me over the table. "Ian was waiting, but for some reason he wanted to wait for you to be killed or brought back before attempting to take over Arrortha. Now that you are here, he's emboldened to attack the castle. The *castle*. Stealing some kid in the middle of the night."

"That *kid* was my brother."

"Be that as it may, we don't have the resources to go looking throughout the entirety of Arrortha for a ten-year-old boy. Even if we were to find him, are we going to march the army against Ian's getting him back?"

"I'll go by myself if I have to," I said.

"That's amusing. You have no training or experience. Maybe we should send you and send the Hamilton boy with you. Such a waste of talent, that one. Then Ian will get what he wants."

"It won't be you who goes. I can't imagine he'll be hiding in the dining area."

I get it; it was a low blow. But I was livid.

Cassius rocketed up, slamming his meaty paws on the table. "Your mouth will kill you much faster than any of Ian's men could. If I were only ten years younger, they'd be dragging your body out of here."

I stood to match him. My Glacies roared to life, and in only a fraction of a second, it had come up with multiple attacks, all of which ended with Cassius regretting what he had started. I was not a confrontational kid; I'd never started any of those fights growing up. But right now, it was taking everything in me to not vault over the table.

"Try it," I said, my pulse thumping in my ears.

His eyes narrowed. "You have no idea who—"

He suddenly brought his hands up over his face, turning away from me, hunching over. The other members of the group, who had been intently watching the altercation, joined him in looking away from me. I flashed back to the bus station in Pittsburgh, where Maya had done the same.

One thing we know is that when you get mad, your eyes will turn white, and it'll freeze anything that makes eye contact with you for too long.

I felt a hand placed lightly on my shoulder, followed by a soft voice.

"Jaden, dear, please take a breath. We're all a little emotional today, but I need you to calm down. Nobody here needs to be frozen today."

Her hand removed itself from my shoulder before she addressed everyone else.

"This meeting is over. The council will discuss the events of last night later, without my son present."

The other members verbally agreed, standing and walking toward the exit, some avoiding eye contact, while others avoided looking at me entirely.

It suited me just fine.

* * *

Half an hour later, I was sitting in the small dining room. I'd since calmed down, but nevertheless, I was left alone. A small spread of food remained from those who had eaten earlier, laid out on silver trays scattered across the table. I looked at the food, but had yet to touch anything.

The door to the dining room opened, and the queen, with Brooke in tow, strolled in. They took seats across the table from me, neither reaching for any of the food. My mother smiled at me, rubbing her temples, the bags under her eyes showing how little she had slept last night, too. Brooke seemed to be refreshed from the night but looked anxiously at her boss.

"Did Ian say anything else to you last night?" my mom asked softly.

"No, just that he wants me to join him. It's all he's ever said. And that—" I trailed off.

"And what?" she asked.

"That taking Ollie is some sort of motivation."

"Motivation?"

"For me. I don't know. It doesn't matter now, anyway. He's gone."

"Look at me, Jaden."

I brought my gaze up to meet hers.

"I have already sent out as many Searchers as I can. They will find him."

"What do I do until then?"

"Be a kid! Go explore the city, though, make sure you take someone with you. Go to the arena and train. But Jaden, it may be a while before we can find him."

I nodded, turning to a platter of muffins, where I grabbed one.

"I have to go. Unfortunately, many people want meetings with the queen, although I'd rather be part of a test hunt than meet with Cassius again."

I grinned despite myself. She grinned back at me, a twinkle of mischief in her eyes.

"Please eat something. I will see you later today. I love you, Jaden."

I watched her go, then turned back to my muffin.

I spent the rest of the morning wandering aimlessly around the castle, opening every door I could find, looking for anything interesting and able to take my mind off Ollie. By late morning, it was obvious I wasn't going to find such a thing, and I began getting restless.

Around lunchtime, I couldn't stand it anymore. I left through the front of the castle, following the path around and behind it, through the field Maya had taken me to yesterday. I sat down on the edge of the cliff, my legs dangling over the edge, looking out over the rolling mountains and Straucka's distant buildings.

Maybe I should go after Ollie myself.

But how? I knew nobody here, or anywhere, for that matter. Outside of Straucka, I knew no other kingdoms, or the distances between them. No, I decided, trained Searchers were Ollie's best chances.

I took in the view, basking in the peace the calm valley brought. Before long, footsteps cut through the soft breeze. I turned to see who was there, as Maya sauntered through the field, the grass crunching under her feet, a soft smile on her face.

"I thought I might find you here," she said, sitting down next to me. After a few moments, she said, "I'm really sorry about Ollie."

I nodded thanks, keeping my attention on the valley.

"Have you made any friends yet?"

I let out a sharp laugh, which made her get defensive.

"I'm being serious. As much as I love this place, you shouldn't be here alone. Especially you. And with what happened last night…." Her voice trailed off.

"Outside of Ollie, I've been alone my whole life."

"I understand that, but you don't have to be. Even when I lost Sofia, I had people there for me."

"Vincent?" I guessed.

She sighed. "Yes. He was my best friend once I lost her."

Silence overtook us again.

"How did I not see it coming?" she asked.

"What do you mean?"

"How did I not see it coming? Vincent always told me that one day he was going to be someone, that he would be respected." She shook her head. "I should've known he'd be dumb enough to believe Ian. I thought I meant more to him than that.

Guess that shows how good I am at judging character," she said with a sarcastic laugh.

That made two of us.

"Can I ask you a question?" she asked, after a while. "What does 'Learn To Dance' mean?"

I looked down at my sweatshirt, where the saying was being rained on by a single cloud. I forgot I'd been wearing it since I arrived, refusing to change it even after showering.

"It's something one of my foster parents said. There was a saying on Earth that if you danced in the rain, then storms weren't so bad."

"Have you ever done it?"

A genuine laugh escaped before I could contain it. "Can't say that I have. I don't really dance much."

"Maybe that's because you've only tried it alone."

She extended her arm slowly, hovering it over my shoulders. I'm sure she was waiting for me to tense, or to even get up and move away. But this time, I didn't stop her. She rested it gently around me as we sat. It felt... weird, like she wasn't trying to deceive me. It was more personal, as if she wanted me to know that she cared with every piece of her. The hair on the back of my neck stood, and I was just hoping she couldn't tell.

"I just wish there was a way I could help Ollie," I said, saying the first thing that would come to mind.

"There is."

I looked at her, a spark of hope reigniting. "How?"

"While we wait, we make sure you're training. Embrace your powers, learn how to use them, and make them work for you. Ian has a point: the strong do thrive here. They will find him, and when they do, we will rescue him."

232

"Okay," I said, nodding. Deep down, I knew she was right... and I knew where to start. I rose to my feet, her arm slipping off my back. I took a few steps back toward the castle, but she stayed seated.

"Are you coming?"

Her face twisted into confusion as she faced me. "To where?"

"I figured I'd go see if the Hamiltons are still at the arena. You said if anyone is going to give me a fight, it's Ky, and Quinn scares me, which I'm sure can only help. The problem is, they're both Glacies, and I think I'm going to need to be healed once or twice."

A smile—a true smile—spread across her face as she sprang to her feet and followed me through the flowers and into the city below.

Acknowledgments

I never thought the acknowledgments section of my first novel would be the hardest part to write, but here we are. Not because I don't have anyone to thank (That whole "It takes a village" saying? Couldn't be more true), but because words are harder when people deserve to know how much they mean to you.

First and foremost, a special thank you to my wife, Claire. Without your support, this never would've happened. From brainstorming to character design, the effort you put into supporting my silly dream is not something I take for granted. Thank you.

To the rest of my family: my mom, dad, and sister — thank you. After you got over the initial "What?" of me revealing the book, your first words were, "What is it about?" and "Can I read it?" For that, I will forever be grateful.

To my editor, Theodora Bryant of Authors' HQ. Without you, this would look a lot different (and way worse). You never sugar-coated things, which I realize is what I needed. You turned what was a rough first draft into something I can feel proud of.

I also owe many thanks to my Aunt Connie and Uncle Oris. You've both been instrumental in the development of this project. From expanding my beta reader list to giving me guidance on how to write in the first place, the lessons you two gave me drove me forward at times where the horizon seemed dim.

To Carson, Case, Graycen, and anyone else who read *The Cursed Heir* before it even had a title. Thank you for giving it a chance. Back when I was too afraid to even admit the work was my own, you took the time to read and give me feedback.

Finally, thank you to anyone who was even remotely the inspiration behind a character. You make the Earth side of the portal worth exploring; you never know what you might uncover.

About the Author

Adam Schrag is a radiation therapist with a passion for people. When he's not at work, he pursues his hobbies such as writing, watching sports, and enjoying nature. He lives with his wife in Manhattan, KS, where they reside with their dog, Gary. He spends his summers coaching high school baseball, where he draws a lot of character inspiration from his players.

www.ingramcontent.com/pod-product-compliance
Lightning Source LLC
Chambersburg PA
CBHW022134240626
47153CB00007B/2357